*Books by Ellen Conford*

IMPOSSIBLE, POSSUM
WHY CAN'T I BE WILLIAM?
DREAMS OF VICTORY

# DREAMS OF VICTORY

# DREAMS OF VICTORY

## by Ellen Conford
### Illustrated by Gail Rockwell

Little, Brown and Company     Boston     Toronto

FIRST EDITION

T 03/73

"There's no business like show business, like no business I know. Ev'rything
about it is appealing. . . ."

"There's no business like show business" by Irving Berlin. © Copyright 1946
Irving Berlin. Reprinted by permission of Irving Berlin Music Corporation.

Library of Congress Cataloging in Publication Data

Conford, Ellen.
    Dreams of Victory.

    SUMMARY: When her day dreams continually conflict
with reality, Victory becomes convinced of her
inferiority. Fortunately, a class essay gives her a
new perspective.
    I.  Rockwell, Gail, illus.  II.  Title.
PZ7.C7593Dr          [Fic]          72-8437
ISBN 0-316-15294-3

*Published simultaneously in Canada
by Little, Brown & Company (Canada) Limited*

PRINTED IN THE UNITED STATES OF AMERICA

To Jill Edelson and Ellen Sarra
and to David and Michael

# DREAMS OF
# VICTORY

# I

"HERE SHE COMES! Here she comes!"
The word was quickly passed around the grand ballroom of the Mark Hanna Hotel, and the excitement grew as the noise of the six hundred victorious election workers drowned out the five-piece band.

"She's coming! She's coming!"

The faithful supporters began to clap rhythmically, and as they clapped, they chanted, "We want Victory, we want Victory!"

Suddenly, the crowd burst into cheers. Victory Benneker was being escorted to the front of the room by her campaign manager and two Secret Service men. Smiling and waving at her followers, she walked to the microphone and looked out at the sea of faces.

She waited for the noise to die down. Finally she raised her hand, and the cheering people managed to quiet themselves to hear what their Victory had to say.

"Ladies and gentlemen," she began. "The people have spoken —"

The crowd burst into cheers again, and it was a moment or two before she could go on.

"You have elected me the first woman President of the United States —"

"VICTORY! VICTORY! VICTORY!" the crowd began to scream. It was several more minutes before she could continue.

"And I promise all of you — I will do my best to make you glad you chose to honor me with this great responsibility."

The band struck up "Happy Days Are Here Again," and the ballroom reverberated with the sounds of people loudly singing along, clapping, stamping their feet, cheering.

Victory leaned toward the microphone.

"I just want to say, thank you all! Thank you for your hard work, and thank you for your support. We couldn't have done it without you! You're the greatest friends a candidate ever had!"

As she stepped off the podium, the crowd surged forward. Flashbulbs popped; her campaign workers surrounded her, struggling to touch her, to shake her hand, to see, close up, her famous smile. . . .

"Vic — Vic — *hey!* Snap out of it, will you?"

"What? Oh, sorry, Jane."

My best friend was waving her hand in front of my eyes.

"Good grief, you've been sitting there staring for ten minutes. You weren't even listening to me."

"Sorry," I said dreamily. "I guess I got carried away."

"You'll get carried away all right if you keep this up. All the way to the Funny Farm, they'll carry you away."

I looked down at my lunch. All that was left was a cellophane strip from the bologna and a lonely crust of bread. I didn't even remember eating it.

"Now listen, Vic, come on. Do you or don't you want me to nominate you for class president? Elections are this afternoon — you have to make up your mind."

I sighed. I never should have told Janey about wanting to run for class president. It was so stupid. Who was going to vote for me? Janey, that's who. And me, myself. That's two. And?

"Look," I began, "do you really think I have a chance? I mean, even the slightest, teeniest chance to win?"

Jane shrugged.

"Why not? Stranger things have happened."

"Oh, thanks a heap."

"I didn't mean it that way," she said. "All I mean

is, it's possible, so why not try? What have you got to lose?"

"My pride," I said glumly. "My lunch, too, maybe."

"Oh, Vic, it's no big thing, it's just a dumb little class election. Nothing to get sick over."

"What if nobody votes for me? What if I don't get one single vote?"

"Well, you have to get one vote at least. I'll vote for you. And besides, it's a secret ballot. You'll never know how many votes you got."

"That's true," I admitted.

"So? What? Yes or no?"

Victory Benneker, first woman president. I was still tingling with pleasure from my imaginary election. That must have been the reason — the only reason — I agreed to let Janey nominate me for class president.

Mrs. Friedman rapped on her desk with a ruler. "Nominations for class president are now in order. We must have the candidates nominated, then we must have another person to second the nomination." I looked at Janey in a panic. I'd forgotten about seconding. *What if no one seconded me?* Oh, no, that would be too much. I would be humiliated in front of everybody. I'd never get over *that*.

I shook my head at Jane. "Don't nominate me, don't do it!" I concentrated on sending my thoughts to her, clenching my teeth and thinking, "No, no, no," over and over again.

Sharon Webb — "Spider" to her closest enemies — raised her hand.

"Yes, Sharon?"

She stood up and brushed a strand of long, blond hair back from her face. Spider Webb has the longest, blondest hair in the whole class, and she makes sure everybody notices.

"I nominate James Fallon," she said.

"Second! Second!" At least five people yelled out before she sat down.

"No, no, no!" I repeated in my head, staring hard at Jane.

Because, even if some miracle happened, and I did get seconded, James Fallon was too much competition for me — or for anyone else, for that matter. He was too smart, too popular, too nice, too much of everything I wasn't. Forget it, Madam President. The world isn't ready for you yet ,r, at least, Class 6-3 isn't. There will be other ▿ ., other elections.

"I nominate ᵛ ᵎ .y Benneker."

Oh, Jane, how could you? How could you?

Silence. *No one was going to second me.* Please, please, let there be a fire drill. An earthquake. A flash flood. A small catastrophe — anything!

"I second."

Good old Mark Vogel. Good, kind, understanding Mark Vogel. Mark is known for his kindness to dumb animals. He's going to be a vet — but someone else will have to give his shots for him. Mark hates to see anyone upset or embarrassed, and I blessed him as I pressed my hand to my stomach, making sure my lunch was going to stay put.

"Are there any other nominations?" Mrs. Friedman asked.

There weren't.

"All right. Write the name of the person you're voting for on a piece of paper, fold it up, and put it in this box. Judy will collect the ballots. Mark and Sharon and Judy and Jane will count the votes."

I tore a little piece of paper from my notebook. I hesitated before writing my own name. I felt kind of funny voting for myself, but if I didn't stick up for me, who would? I mean, after all, it was probably going to be embarrassing enough. I had to hold on to at least a shred of self-respect.

"Victory Benneker," I wrote, then crossed it out and wrote, "Vicky Benneker." Then I crumpled up that piece of paper so no one would see that I'd crossed out "Victory" and I tore out another piece of paper and printed VICKY BENNEKER in block letters.

By this time, Judy was next to my desk with the ballot box, and I folded up my ballot and dropped it in. I hoped it wouldn't be *too* lonely in there.

When all the ballots were collected, the four vote counters went to the back of the room to add up the results.

I sat, miserable, in my seat, hoping they wouldn't give the actual numbers, but just announce that James Fallon had won, and leave it at that. I mean, what if they said, "Vicky Benneker — two, James Fallon — twenty-four?" Oh, no, they wouldn't do that.

Would they?

"Okay, we're finished," Sharon Webb announced.

"Good," said Mrs. Friedman. "Who is our new class president?"

"Tum ta da dum!" sang Kenny Clark, imitating a trumpet fanfare.

"James Fallon," Sharon said importantly.

"Congratulations, James," said Mrs. Friedman.

"Well, I hope we've profited by our mini-lesson in democratic elections."

Oh, yes, definitely. I certainly profited from this little experience. It was very educational. I loved every minute of my defeat. And I want to thank you all for not voting for me, because I didn't want the stupid job anyway. So there.

"Too bad," said Jane, as we walked out to the school bus.

"I didn't want you to nominate me in the first place," I grumbled. "Or at least, in the second place — after I found out about the seconding, and James Fallon."

"Well, you didn't tell me that," Janey said.

"I tried, I really did. You just didn't receive my thought waves."

"Thought waves?" repeated Jane, puzzled.

"Never mind. Listen, just tell me one thing. How much of a landslide was it?"

"Oh, what difference does it make?" Jane said. "I don't even remember."

"Yes you do," I insisted. "Was it that bad?"

"Honest," Jane lied, "I don't remember. I'm sure it wasn't exactly a landslide."

"An avalanche?" I suggested.

We got on the bus. Sharon Webb was right behind us.

"Look," said Jane, "it's a dumb job anyway. It's nothing to get miserable about. Class president — big deal. He gets to close the windows at three o'clock. And when they collect for Red Cross, he probably gets to carry around the container. Wow, what an honor."

"Oh, it's not that, and you know it," I protested.

"Tough luck, Vicky," said Spider Webb sweetly, leaning over the back of our seat.

"Yeah. Well," I said, "your candidate won. Congratulations."

Spider played with a strand of her hair, rubbing it lovingly between two fingers. I tried to picture her bald.

"Oh, you didn't do so badly," Sharon said casually.

"Sharon!" Janey warned.

"You got six votes." And Spider sat back in her seat as the bus started up.

Six votes. I felt tears coming to my eyes, and tried to blink them away. No matter how much you tell yourself no one will vote for you, you don't really believe it, I guess, until you come right up and face it. I knew I'd lose, and I knew I'd lose by a lot, but now I really, *officially*, knew it.

"Listen," Jane whispered, "it was only because it was Jimmy. Anyone else, and —"

"Oh, I know, I know. Don't worry about me. I'm really glad she told me." I rubbed my eyes with the back of my hand. "Actually, I'm delighted. It's four more votes than I expected."

# II

M Y MOTHER was in the kitchen rolling out a pie crust when I got home. My mother is a kindergarten teacher and makes the world's worst pies. But every once in a while she decides to do something old-fashioned and motherly like in the TV commercials, so she bakes pies. Then my father and I have to eat her pies and say they're delicious, and then she goes and makes more pies because we like pies so much.

"Hi, dear," she said as I came into the kitchen. "How was school?"

"Okay," I said, taking some milk from the refrigerator. "What kind of a pie are you making?"

"Peach," she said proudly.

"Oh boy," I said. She'd never made a peach pie before. I could feel my stomach already preparing to go on strike.

I looked down at the crust she was rolling out. It looked a little strange.

"Hey," I said. "Why is that crust gray?"

"Oh, well, I ran out of regular flour, and I had some

of that rye flour left from the time I tried to bake rye bread, so I'm using that instead."

"Rye pie?" I gulped.

"Rye pie!" She grinned. "That's funny."

"Mom," I began, pouring myself some milk, "why did you name me Victory?"

"Oh, dear," she sighed, wiping her forehead with floury fingers. "Here we go again."

"But, with all the names in the world —"

"I've told you at least a thousand times," she said, "and you keep asking me."

"I keep waiting for you to give me a *good* reason," I said grimly.

"Because I waited so long to have a child," she said, "that just having you born was sort of a victory; and then, as soon as you were born, I knew that you'd be Something — I could see it in your eyes. And I wanted to give you a name that meant success, and achievement . . . so I named you Victory."

"Same old reasons again," I said.

"Because they're the truth," my mother replied.

"You should have named me Defeat," I said sourly. "It fits me better."

"That's a terrible thing to say!" my mother scolded.

"It's a good name for a loser."

"But you're not a loser," she objected, opening a can of peach pie filling.

"That's what you think. We had elections for class president today."

"Oh, I see," she nodded.

"No you don't," I said. "I haven't told you yet."

"You lost one class election," my mother said, "and that makes you a loser?"

"I got six votes!" I cried. "Six votes, out of twenty-six kids in the class. You know what that means?"

"That means," my mother said calmly, "that you feel rotten, and you think nobody likes you."

"I hate it when you understand me all the time," I said sulkily. My mother tried to hide a smile, but she couldn't, and then it even sounded funny to me, and I started to giggle.

She grinned back at me and began lifting the pie crust into the baking dish. But the crust would not come off the pastry board in one piece, so she had to sort of scrape it off and then press it into the pie plate in little lumps.

"There. That doesn't look too bad, does it?"

Next she took the can of peach pie filling and poured it into the pie plate.

"Where's the top crust?" I asked.

"Oh, well, I didn't have enough flour for two crusts. This is a one-crust pie."

"Why don't you make one of those crisscross tops?" I suggested. "You know, with the strips going back and forth? I bet you have enough left over dough for that."

"Listen," my mother snapped, wiping her fingers on a dish towel, "you're lucky to get a one-crust pie. I have enough trouble making the bottom crust without standing here and cutting out little strips and weaving them back and forth —"

"Okay, okay," I said apologetically. "It just looks kind of naked that way, that's all."

"Naked?" my mother repeated coldly. "I never would have thought of it as naked. If you've got nothing better to do than stand here and criticize —"

"No, no, forget it," I said hastily. "I'll go do my homework." So I won't have to look at that naked pie, I added silently.

My father got home early because all the electricity in his office building went off.

"What is that smell?" he asked, sniffing as he hung up his coat. "Your mother isn't trying to bake bread again?"

"No. That's a pie."

"A pie? It doesn't smell like a pie. Not even one of hers." He said that last part under his breath, but I heard him.

"Well," I explained, "she was out of regular flour, so she used rye flour."

My father clamped his hand down on my shoulder — hard.

"I'm sure," he said firmly, "it will be delicious."

The rest of the dinner wasn't bad, really, but thinking about my mother's pie kind of spoiled it.

"And for dessert," she said, placing it on the table with a dramatic flourish, "a homemade peach pie."

"Yippee," I whispered. My father glared at me.

We all looked down at the pie. The edge of the crust was dark brown. The rest of the crust was gray. The peaches had shriveled up in the oven, and looked wrinkled and dry.

"Well, it doesn't look very pretty," my mother admitted.

"Who cares how it looks?" my father said loyally. "It's how it tastes that counts."

My mother cut us each a piece. I think she had a little trouble getting it cut, but she didn't say so.

"It's so — dry," I said weakly.

"But delicious!" my father added quickly.

The phone rang.

"I'll get it!" I shouted, and leaped up before anyone could stop me.

"Hello?"

"Hi, Vicky, this is Jane. Did Judy call you?"

"Judy? No, what about?"

"She's having a party next Saturday. It's her birthday."

"Maybe she isn't inviting me," I said glumly. "I wouldn't be surprised."

"Oh, stop feeling so sorry for yourself. I think you're still brooding over that dumb election. Anyway, she is inviting you, because she told me she is. And you know who else she's inviting?"

"Who?" I asked.

"Boys."

"Boys?" I repeated. "Why does she want to do a thing like that?"

"I don't know," Jane said. "Well, listen, maybe she's trying to call you now, so I'll hang up."

"Okay," I said. " 'Bye."

I put the phone down and walked slowly back into the kitchen.

"Sit down and finish your pie, honey," said my mother. "Who was that?"

"Janey. Judy Olivera is going to have a birthday party. With *boys*."

"Oh, how nice!" my mother beamed. "We'll get you a new dress. When is it?"

"Next Saturday. Hey!" I said, with a sudden burst of inspiration, "I'm getting kind of fat. Before we go shopping I'd better lose some weight."

"But you're not fat at all," my mother argued.

"Oh, yes, I am. Can't you see how fat I'm getting? I'm going on a diet."

I pushed my pie plate away and stood up. My father looked at me suspiciously.

"Excuse me, please. I'm expecting a phone call any minute. Call me," I said to my mother, "if you want help with the dishes."

Judy called about half an hour later.

After she told me I was invited to her party, I tried to find out, as politely as I could, why she'd asked boys.

"Oh, my mother thought it would be fun. You know, games, dancing —"

Dancing!

"She thought it would be good practice for when I'm older."

Oh, brother.

When I hung up, I wandered back into the kitchen. My mother had just loaded the dishwasher and my father was about to take out the garbage.

"There's going to be dancing," I announced disgustedly.

"Dancing?" my mother echoed.

"At Judy's party. *Dancing*."

"Oh. That should be nice."

"Nice? What's nice about it? It's dumb. I don't know how to dance."

"You can learn," my father said, as he went out the back door with the garbage.

"Oh, sure," I grumbled. "The last three times I tried to learn, Janey told me to forget it."

"Really," my mother said, "it's not hard. Now, for instance, the fox-trot —"

"Mom," I said, "I don't think they do the fox-trot much any more."

My father came back inside.

"Oh, dear, I guess not," she said, wrinkling up her forehead. "Too bad — such a lovely dance. I don't suppose you want to learn the cha-cha either?"

"No."

"You know, at the wedding we went to last month," my father said, "everybody was doing the twist and the cha-cha —"

"Not everybody," I said. "Just the old people."

"I resent that," my father said.

"Oh, you know what I mean."

"She's right," my mother sighed. "They don't dance the way we used to."

"Well, what am I going to do?" I wailed.

"Maybe," my mother suggested, "you could ask Jane —"

"Oh, she's sick of trying to teach me."

"She won't mind," my father said. "It'll make her feel good that you asked her help."

"I'll bet," I said.

The next day, after school, Janey came over to teach me how to dance. Again.

The lesson was not what you'd call a rousing success.

"Now look, Vic," she said, bouncing around to a record she'd brought with her, "it's all in the hips and knees. You hardly have to move your feet at all."

I tried to copy what she was doing, but I felt like an elephant with a charley horse.

"No, no, not like that!"

"Well, I can't help it," I cried. "My knees don't move that way."

"Don't be ridiculous. All it takes is a little coordination."

"Which I haven't got. Oh, Jane, it's hopeless."

"It is *not* hopeless," Jane said sternly.

"You said yourself it was hopeless last time," I pointed out.

"Forget what I said," Jane ordered. "Now, watch me. You put your arms like this . . ."

I put my arms like that.

"Then you just kind of do this with your knees . . ."

An hour later my mother came upstairs to see how the lesson was going.

"Forget it," I told her.

"What's the matter?"

"She's having a little trouble with her hips," Jane said.

"A little trouble?" I shrieked. "Why don't you be honest and tell her that I'm a hopeless case, and if you broke both my legs I couldn't do any worse."

"Well, sometimes it takes a while before you catch on," my mother said sympathetically.

"Mother, I will *never* catch on."

And that was the absolutely final end of my dancing lessons.

# III

WHEN MY MOTHER took me shopping for a dress to wear to Judy's party, we found that I had grown into the next size. I'd gained four pounds on my fake diet. And it didn't help any when the salesgirl tried to steer us to "something in navy blue — dark colors are so slimming."

"It's for a party," my mother said firmly. "We want something in party colors."

The dress we finally got was red, white and blue, and it was really very nice. But on Saturday night I felt *fat*.

"Hey, that's a really wild dress," Janey said, when her mother dropped her off at my house before the party.

"You like it?"

"Yeah. You look like a patriot."

"A fat patriot," I said. "I told my mother I was gaining weight so I wouldn't have to eat one of her pies. And then I really did get fat."

"Oh, you don't look fat at all," Jane argued. "It's your imagination."

"Well, maybe I have a fat imagination."

My father drove us to Judy's house at seven-thirty.

"Come in, come in," beamed Mrs. Olivera, as she answered our knock. "Everyone's down in the family room."

The "family room" is the Oliveras' basement.

Janey and I went downstairs. The place was decorated with crepe-paper streamers and balloons. Mark Vogel was blowing up balloons and Kenny Clark was breaking them.

"Hi!" said Judy, waving to us as we came down the stairs.

We put our presents on a table with the other presents.

Mark Vogel handed Judy a balloon to hang up.

Kenny Clark broke another ballon. It looked like a losing battle.

"Please don't break any more balloons, Kenny," Judy said. "We're running out."

Kenny threw a potato chip at Jane.

By quarter to eight, everyone else had come, and Judy's mother and father decided to have what they called an "icebreaker" game. The idea was to get all the boys, who were on one side of the room, and all the girls, on the other side, mixed up together.

"Now, all the girls, take off one shoe," said Mrs. Olivera, "and put it in the center of the room."

When there was a big pile of shoes on the floor, Mrs. Olivera said, "Now each boy pick up a shoe and find the girl it fits."

That didn't take too long. Kenny Clark found my shoe. He threw it at me.

"Now the girl whose shoe you found is your partner for the first dance," Mrs. Olivera announced.

There were howls of protest from the boys, who immediately left the girls they were with and collected on the other side of the room again.

Mrs. Olivera frowned and bit her lip.

"Now, come on, boys," she urged. "Don't be shy."

Kenny Clark threw a pretzel at Jimmy Fallon.

Mr. Olivera put on a record. Sharon Webb walked over to the clump of boys and said, "Come on, Mark. We'll dance."

Mark kind of hung back and shook his head. "I don't know how," he mumbled.

"I'll show you. It's easy." She grabbed his hand, and started to move in time to the music. "Just copy what I do."

Jerking her hips and knees, and swinging her long blond hair around, she danced the way Janey had showed me, but her movements were a little different, and she looked just like a professional dancer on television. At first, Mark seemed self-conscious and just sort of stood there, but after a while he started to imitate her motions, and really caught on. Even the boys who had been snickering stopped and watched, and Mark began to look like he was actually enjoying himself.

When the record was over, Jimmy Fallon wandered over to Sharon and said, "Hey, that's pretty good. You want to show me how to do it?"

"Sure," said Spider, brushing her hair away from her eyes. I tried to picture her with a crew cut.

The music started up again, and Jimmy, who isn't shy at all, learned even faster than Mark.

In half an hour, Spider had taught almost every boy in the room how to dance. The only thing was, after they danced with Spider, they went back together to huddle in their corner. Mrs. Olivera didn't like that at all.

"Now that you boys know how to dance," she said, "we can have our special-event dances."

How I wished Judy's mother could think of something besides dancing! There's more to life, I thought grimly, than shaking yourself in time to music with a dumb boy standing opposite you. The whole thing was definitely not worth the trouble.

"The first event," Mrs. Olivera went on, "is the broom dance. Now, there's an extra boy, so he has to dance with the broom. Whenever the music stops, you must all change partners and the boy left without a partner has to dance with the broom. Okay now, get a partner — *quick!*"

The boys didn't move.

"Okay," she said, changing her tactics. "Girls, *you* pick partners."

All the girls, who'd been sitting around eating potato chips for half an hour while Spider Webb taught the boys to dance, charged over to the boys' side of the room and grabbed a partner. I was the slowest to pick, because I really didn't want to dance at all, so there were only two boys left by the time I got around to it. One was Kenny Clark, so I chose the other one, Mickey Michaelson. Kenny looked delighted when Mrs. Olivera handed him the broom.

The music started and Mickey turned out to be almost as rotten at dancing as I was. Only he didn't think so.

Kenny jumped around with the broom, bumping into people and showing off, pretending he was kissing the broom, and things like that. When the music stopped, all the boys raced toward Spider, and all the girls stood around waiting for someone to pick them after Spider was taken. Kenny didn't even try to get a partner. He just held onto his broom.

"Now, Kenny, that's not fair," Mrs. Olivera scolded. "You have to try and get a partner."

"But I like the broom," he protested. "She's the best dancer here."

Finally Mrs. Olivera gave up trying to make social successes out of us and said it was time for Judy to open her presents. All the girls watched Judy open her presents. All the boys ate potato chips and drank soda and pushed into each other over in their corner of the room.

Then Mrs. Olivera turned off the lights and brought in Judy's birthday cake with all the candles lit. Everybody sang "Happy Birthday," and Judy blew out the candles. Kenny Clark sang, "Happy birthday to you, you belong in a zoo, you look like a monkey and you act like one too," and all the boys laughed.

After the ice cream and cake, Spider and a couple of the other girls got some boys to dance with them. I sat next to the phonograph and looked at Judy's records. Nobody asked me to dance. But I didn't care, I told myself. I was glad to have the chance to sit down without Mrs. Olivera screaming, "Dance, dance, everybody dance!" like some kind of fanatic.

I mean, who wanted to dance? Especially with those dumb boys. I'd probably have ended up with my toes broken. Who needed it? That's what I told myself as I sat there and waited for the party to end.

Finally parents started to come to pick up the kids, and Mrs. Olivera called down that my father was there, so I yelled to Jane, who was dancing with Mark, that it was time to go. She actually looked disappointed.

"How was the party?" my father asked as we drove off.

"Pretty good," Janey said breathlessly. "Boy, all that dancing wears you out."

"I wouldn't know about that," I said coldly.

We dropped Jane off at her house and drove home. When we got in, my mother was watching television.

"How was the party?" she asked.

"All right," I replied glumly.

"Did you dance?"

"Once," I said.

"Oh," she said.

I flopped down next to her on the couch; she was watching the Miss Galaxy Beauty Pageant. I was pretty tired, and my new dress felt tight and crumpled. The contestants on the screen were parading up and down in evening gowns. They looked cool and crisp and skinny. They smiled a lot. I sighed and closed my eyes.

". . . And now, ladies and gentlemen, the tenth semifinalist in the Miss Galaxy contest, from Oakvale, Long Island, Miss Victory Benneker!"

She gasped, and Miss Thailand kissed her while everyone clapped wildly. She glided down stage toward the emcee, Bob Baker. Victory brushed her long blond hair out of her eyes and smiled warmly at the audience.

"Congratulations, semifinalists. And now, in just a few minutes," Bob Baker announced, "we'll have the all-important talent competition. Then the judges will pick the five finalists, one of whom will be Miss Galaxy for 1981."

Moments later Victory was dressed in her costume awaiting her turn to perform. She was to go on last, and it was nerve-racking waiting backstage for all the others to finish their acts.

Finally she heard Bob Baker say, "And now, from Oakvale, Long Island, Miss New York, Victory Benneker, will do a number called 'Dance Through the Ages.'"

"You're on, Victory," whispered Mrs. Fanning, the pageant coordinator. "Good luck!"

The curtain opened, the orchestra struck up "The Charleston" and she danced on stage to cheers of admiration from the audience. From the jazzy rhythms of the Charleston, Victory swept into a slow, dramatic tango, and as the audience applauded, she switched again to a fast, complicated solo version of the jitterbug, which the crowd really loved. Changing pace once more, she swayed to the Latin tempo of a mambo. The audience, mostly older people, loved that, because it reminded them of the good old days, when they danced at parties and weddings and things. Last, Victory swung into a loud, fast rock number, her long blond hair flying, her body rocking to the beat, her heart pounding wildly to the cheers of the crowd.

When it was over, she stood, head bowed, arms at her sides, stunned by the thunderous storm of applause that filled the auditorium. Victory walked off stage, but when Bob Baker came out, they were still applauding and finally he had to call her back out to take another bow.

"Well, Victory," he smiled, "I guess these people know a dancer when they see one."

She bowed and threw kisses at the audience, and after she left the stage again, they began to quiet down.

It was time to pick the five finalists.

They were back in their evening gowns again, and everyone was saying they were sure Victory would win. She kept smiling and thanking people. Miss Denmark hugged her, and the pageant coordinator kept patting everybody's shoulders reassuringly.

"And the fifth finalist, from Oakvale, Long Island . . ."

The cheering began even before he got her name out, and built to a wild peak as she stepped forward.

"You sure are their favorite," Miss Japan whispered.

Then they paraded up and down the runway one last time, as the judges marked their choices.

"The time has come, ladies and gentlemen. This is what we've all been waiting for. The judges have picked the four runners-up, and the new Miss Galaxy, and here is their decision."

The drums began a slow, dramatic rumble.

"The fourth runner-up: Miss Italy! The third runner-up: Miss Scotland! The second runner-up: Miss West Berlin!"

There were only two finalists left! Miss Japan and Victory clasped hands and smiled excitedly at each other. The suspense was unbearable. They trembled as they stood together, waiting.

"The first runner-up: Miss Japan —"

That left Victory! Miss Japan hugged her, everyone was screaming and the audience went wild with joy. She was hugged, kissed, pushed and pulled to the center of the stage. She couldn't believe it was really happening, and her knees felt like they'd turned to Jell-O. She'd won! Victory Benneker was the new Miss Galaxy!

"Congratulations, Miss Galaxy!" Bob Baker said. He put an ermine cloak around her shoulders, and last year's Miss Galaxy placed a diamond crown on her head. Tears streamed down Victory's cheeks as Mrs. Fanning handed her a bouquet of roses.

"Now, Miss Galaxy, meet your loyal subjects. And weren't they with you, all the way!"

It was pandemonium. She walked down the long runway slowly, the tears dripping on her American Beauty roses as the cheers of the audience overwhelmed her. Waving, throwing kisses, blinking as the flashbulbs popped off one after another, she hardly knew what was happening. Could it possibly be real? Could this be Victory Benneker?

She saw her mother in the audience, and her father. They were holding hands, and her mother was crying. She threw them a kiss. She saw Janey, and Mark and all the kids in her class clapping and yelling. Spider was there too. She looked jealous.

Victory, Victory, the whole auditorium throbbed with the sound of her name, and at last it meant something real. A victory for Victory, Victory, Victory . . .

"Victory!" My mother was shaking my shoulder.

"You must be exhausted," she said. "You fell asleep right here. You'd better get to bed, dear."

The late news was on. I nodded. I really was tired. I dragged myself upstairs. My wrinkled dress was a sticky reminder that I was only Victory Benneker, the kid with short brown hair and two left feet.

As I trudged toward my room, I heard the newscaster say, "And in Center City tonight, they chose the new Miss Galaxy. She is nineteen-year-old —"

But my mother clicked off the television, and I didn't catch the name.

# IV

THE SIGNS were all over town.

## GIANT CARNIVAL
# COMING!
## OCTOBER 27
### Games! Rides! Thrills & Chills!

Sponsored by
The Oakvale Chamber of Commerce
to benefit their Youth League

"You want to go?" Jane asked. "My mother said I could, if someone else would come with me. It's at night."

"Sure," I said. "I could use some thrills and chills."

At school, all the kids were talking about the carnival.

"It's about *time* something interesting happened here," Judy Olivera said loudly. "You could spend your whole life in Oakvale and never —"

"My father," cut in Sharon Webb importantly, "who just happens to be the president of the Oakvale Chamber of Commerce —"

"No kidding!" shouted Kenny Clark. Spider never said "my father" without adding, "president of the Chamber of Commerce." Someday they would elect a new president, and poor Spider would have to find something else to call her father. Of course, vice president of the First National Bank of Oakvale (which is what he is) doesn't sound too bad either.

"My father," Spider went on, ignoring Kenny, "says that this carnival is going to be the biggest thing that ever hit this town."

"Gol-lee," said Kenny Clark in his hillbilly voice.

But everybody else was impressed.

"Really?" Judy said. "*That* big?"

"Just this morning my father said to me, 'Sharon, you be sure and tell your friends not to miss this carnival, because it's going to be the biggest thing that ever hit this town.' "

"You said that already," I pointed out.

But nobody was listening to me.

"My father says —"

"She says that a lot, doesn't she?" I murmured to Jane. Jane just nodded and said, "Shh!"

"— going to have the second biggest Ferris wheel in the world."

"Oh boy!" Even Kenny Clark was excited now. "That's for me!"

I tried to remember the last carnival I went to, but for some reason I couldn't remember *any* carnival I went to. Isn't that weird — maybe I'd never been to a carnival in my life. Incredible, but true: a normal, eleven-year-old American girl who had never gone to a real carnival.

From books and TV, I knew a carnival had rides and games, and people throwing balls at milk bottles and men yelling, "Try your strength, ring the bell with the hammer," and things like that, but I had never really seen a carnival with my own eyes, or smelled one with my own nose.

Spider was still talking when the bell rang. Everyone was gathered around her and no one even noticed the bell. She stroked her blond hair, brushing it behind one ear. She loves it when she's the center of attention. It brings out all her best qualities, like conceitedness, show-off-iness, boastfulness, snootiness . . . I tried to picture her with her finger in a light socket, all her hair standing out from her head, straight up, like in the cartoons.

"There's a carnival coming on Saturday!" I yelled, as I slammed the front door and ran into the dining room.

"Hello to you, too," said my mother, looking up from the newspaper.

"Oh — hello. Can I go? Can I?"

Suddenly it was very important to me to go to a real carnival.

"When is it?"

"I *told* you — Saturday. Night."

"At night?" she repeated doubtfully.

"I'll be going with Jane. *Please.*"

"Wait till your father comes home. We'll talk about it then."


My father frowned.

"I don't like the idea of you wandering around at night —"

"I *won't* be wandering around!" I wailed. "And the whole *class* is going to be there, I'll bet. If I don't go, I'll be the *only one* in the *whole class* —"

"*However,*" my father interrupted loudly, "since you won't be alone . . ."

I finally realized they were going to let me go. Why they have to make you suffer before they say yes, I'll never understand.

It turned out that my father, who had said he would drive Jane and me to the carnival, also had to drive Judy Olivera and — yecchh — Spider Webb. See, I said I'd go with Jane, and Jane said Judy wanted to come too, and Spider said she'd go with Judy, etc., etc.

The other thing on our minds besides the carnival was Halloween, which was only four days away. The thing was, no one had made up their mind yet whether or not they were going out trick or treating. Last year when we were ten, it was one thing, but this year, when we were eleven, we kind of wondered if we were too old.

"Kid stuff," Spider said firmly. "Halloween is for little kids."

"I took a poll," Janey announced, "and the results are: All the boys I asked are going, and they're all dressing like hoboes. All the girls I asked haven't decided yet, except Lyn Lombardi, who's taking her little brother around for the first time, and she's dressing like a hobo."

"What's he dressing like?" I asked.

"He's wearing pajamas with feet and going as a rabbit," Jane said.

"Look!" Judy shouted.

We could see the carnival now, the lights blazing, the rides going, and we could hear music and laughter and shouting all mixed up together.

"Mmm," Spider sighed dreamily, "I can smell the hot dogs already."

"You can not!" Judy retorted.

"I have a very sensitive nose," Spider said haughtily.

"Yeah," I giggled, "she smells good."

We drove into the parking lot and my father stopped to let us out.

"Now remember," he said firmly, "I'll meet you at the entrance gate at ten-thirty. You all stick together and be there on time."

"We will, we will!"

Inside the gate we stopped for a minute to argue about what to do first.

"Let's go on the Ferris wheel!" Judy said.

"I'm hungry," I said.

"There's a wheel of fortune," said Spider, "and if you pick the right number you can win a portable stereo set."

"Why don't we just start here and work our way down?" said Janey. That sounded logical, so we agreed to just stop wherever it looked interesting.

But there were booths and games on all sides of us, and everyone who ran a game was yelling, "*Try your luck! Even a baby can win a prize! Everybody wins! Nobody loses! Only a quarter!*" We kept running from one side to the other — *everything* looked interesting.

"I'm going to try this," Jane said, as we came to a booth where you had to break balloons with darts.

"Three tries for a quarter," the man said. "Break three balloons and you pick any prize on the top row.

Break two balloons and you get anything on the second row. Even if you only break one balloon you win a prize. Try your luck, try your skill, ladies."

Well, that didn't look too hard. And on the top row he had transistor radios, cameras, lots of expensive stuff.

"I'm going to try too," I said.

Jane went first. She put down a quarter and the man gave her three darts.

The first one she threw didn't even get near a balloon.

"Too bad, too bad, girlie," the man said, "but you can still win a nice prize."

Well, not all that nice, because from the top row to the second row, the quality of the prizes really plummeted. Like, the second row had some dolls, and stuffed animals, and a plastic duck, stuff like that.

Anyway, with the second dart, Janey broke a balloon.

"*Yay!!*" Judy and I yelled.

"*She wins a prize, she wins a prize!*" the man shouted, so that all the people passing by stopped to look at his booth.

"*Anybody can win, anybody can win! Just watch this little girl, folks!*"

"He's trying to make you nervous so you won't hit another one," I whispered to Jane.

Jane looked sideways at the man and squinted her eyes.

"Oh, he is, eh?" She took her third dart, and pressed her lips together tightly. Concentrating, her eyes narrowed to slits, she leaned forward and hurled the dart at the balloon board. She missed.

"Aww, too bad, girlie, but you still win a prize. Try again, try again. You've got the hang of it now." Jane shook her head.

"Pick your prize, anything from the bottom shelf. *We have a winner here! Pick a prize, anything at all* (from the bottom shelf)." The stuff on the bottom was pretty dreary, but Jane managed to find a red bead necklace, and the man slipped it over her head.

Now it was my turn. I put down my quarter and got the darts. The first one missed by an inch. The second one hit a balloon that was already broken. The third one missed completely, not even hitting the board the balloons were attached to.

"Rats," I grumbled, "it takes you a while to get the feel of it." I plunked down another quarter.

"You only have three dollars," Janey whispered.

"I know, I know," I shushed her.

"Come on," Spider said impatiently. "This is too hard."

I picked up my first dart and took careful aim. Pop! *"We have another winner!"* the man shouted.

The second dart. Whoosh — pop!

"A *double winner, folks! Trying for the big prize! Watch this little girl, everybody!*"

"Now, don't let him shake you up," Janey warned.

I shook my head. I was onto his tricks. Aim, steady now, don't think of that transistor radio up there, just concen — zoom! The dart flew out of my hand and hit — nothing.

"Aww," everybody moaned.

"Try it again, girlie. You're a real pro!" the man urged. "*We have a winner!!*" he yelled. "*Pick anything you want* (from the second shelf)."

I picked a very small purple stuffed dog. It was sort of cute, and it had an orange ribbon around its neck.

"That'll look nice on your bed," Janey said.

A little further on we saw the wheel of fortune.

"Oh, wow," said Judy. "I want to try that! Look at what you can win!"

There were really great prizes — the portable stereo, Polaroid cameras, am-fm radios . . .

"Boy!" Judy cried, digging into her pocket for money.

"Try your luck, girls, win a fabulous prize!"

"Hey, it's fifty cents," Jane said. "That's pretty expensive for one chance."

"But look at what you can *win!*" Judy said.

"You won't find better prizes than these in the

whole midway," the woman behind the booth said. "Try your luck. Only fifty cents to win a fifty-dollar prize."

You had to put your money on a number, and there was a big gold and red wheel with numbers on it. If you picked the right number, you won. Well, it looked like a pretty slim chance that you'd pick the right number, but if you did . . .

We all plunked down our coins on different numbers and the woman spun the wheel.

*"Here she goes, here she goes, round and round, round and round!"* My money was on number 37, and as the wheel spun around, fast at first, then slowing down, slower and slower, I felt my heart thump wildly. Closer, closer, the numbers clicked by, 35 . . . 36 . . . 37 . . .

I shrieked, "Look!" but the wheel didn't stop — 38 . . . 39.

"Ohhh," I groaned. "I almost won."

"I'm going to try again," Judy said.

Jane shook her head.

"Not me," she whispered. "This is a gyp. I'll bet nobody ever wins."

Judy tried twice more, and Sharon too, but they didn't even come close.

Disgusted, Judy walked away.

"What a racket," she sneered.

We stopped to get hot dogs, and then found ourselves in a big area where the rides were.

"There's the Ferris wheel!" Spider shouted.

"Wow!" Judy gasped.

It was huge. You couldn't even see the people in the little cages at the top, it was so big. You could hear them yelling and screaming, though.

It was stopping. As each compartment came around to the bottom, the operator opened the door and let the people step down. One woman got out with her husband and two little kids, and staggered toward us.

"Was *that fun!*" one kid yelled.

"I wanna go again, I wanna go again!" the other one kept screaming.

"Oh, my God," the woman mumbled. "Oh, my God . . ."

All of a sudden I knew I couldn't get on that Ferris wheel. I looked up at the top, and I could see myself in the cage up there, and I could see the cable snap, and I could see the cage falling, falling, plunging to the ground with me in it, screaming. . . .

"Hey! That was great!"

Kenny Clark, Mark Vogel and Jimmy Fallon were piling out of one of the little cages.

"You've got to go on that," Kenny said. "That is really something!"

"Let's go!" Judy said.

"Come on, Vic." Jane tugged at my arm.

I shook my head. "I don't want to."

"Why not?" asked Spider. "It's the second biggest —"

"Yeah, yeah, I know. I just don't feel like it."

"Chicken!" Kenny yelled. "Chicken Vicky, Chicky Vicky!"

"Shut up," I said weakly.

"I'm going again," Kenny said. "Come on, guys."

All the kids got on the Ferris wheel in two cages.

I stood there alone, watching as the Ferris wheel slowly started to go around, taking them higher and higher toward the top. I didn't really believe anything would happen to them — it was just that I couldn't picture myself going way up there to the top, and coming down alive.

But now they'd all make fun of me, because I was afraid.

I never even knew I was a chicken, until I saw that Ferris wheel. That's what made it so awful. I mean, if everyone knew I was a coward all along, that would be one thing. Then they wouldn't expect me to go on the Ferris wheel. But now they all knew something I hadn't even known myself, and Kenny Clark would tell everybody who didn't already know, and everyone would call me Chicken Vicky.

I felt rotten standing there all alone, like everyone

had left me because no one wanted to be with me — and when they got down, they'd all probably talk about the Ferris wheel and ignore me because I hadn't been on it with them.

I stared up at the sky, past the Ferris wheel. The bright lights of the carnival blotted out the stars, but there was a big golden moon. It was the harvest moon, I guessed, or was it the hunter's moon? I thought I could almost make out the craters, the surface was so bright and clear. . . .

# VICTORY I NEARS MOON

*First Woman Astronaut*
*Prepares for Lunar Landing!*
*Victory Says, "A Thrilling Ride!"*

Victory Benneker, the first woman astronaut to be sent on a lunar landing mission, will touch down on the surface of the moon in her LEM, named "Victory I," at 12.32 EST tomorrow morning. Scientists at the Manned Space Center in Houston said that everything is "A-OK" and that both Victories — the LEM and the astronaut — are doing their jobs to perfection.

In a televised transmission yesterday, Victory answered questions by reporters, explained how some of the equipment worked, and gave a demonstration of how to function in a weightless environment. When one reporter asked, "Aren't you nervous at all? You seem so cool!" Victory replied, "I know you'll find this hard to believe, but I used to be a very nervous person. Do you know that I was once too scared to go on a Ferris wheel?"

Mr. and Mrs. Lawrence Benneker, the parents of the astronaut, told reporters that they were certainly proud of their daughter, but not surprised.

"Why do you think we named her Victory?" Mrs. Benneker smiled.

"Wow, that was great!" Jane said. "You really should have tried it, Vic."

I came back to earth with a thud. The kids were getting off the Ferris wheel, laughing and noisy, except for Judy.

"That was really wild," Jimmy Fallon grinned. "I could go on *again*."

"What's the matter, Judy?" Mark asked, as she leaned against the ticket booth.

"I'm nauseous," Judy groaned.

"Aww, poor Judy," Kenny tsked. "You should have stayed down on the ground, with Chicken Vicky."

"Oh, shut up," she whimpered. "I feel *nauseous*."

"Come on," said Janey, "we'll walk around for a while, you'll feel better."

We played some more of the games, and the boys followed along with us. Kenny Clark kept calling me Chicken Vicken, or Chicky Vicky, and when I finally hit him in the shoulder, he grabbed his arm and said, "Ooh, she's killin' me, she's killin' me, make her stop, ooh, ooh!" and hopped around like some dumb little kid.

Jimmy Fallon knocked a pile of milk bottles down with a baseball, and won a big stuffed rabbit which he said he was going to give to his little sister, Francine; but Spider kept saying what a beautiful rabbit it was, and she wished she had a big brother to win a rabbit like that for her, and boy, was Francine lucky. So Jimmy finally said, "Here, if you like it so much," and shoved it at her.

She grinned happily, like a cat; I never knew she was that sneaky, or that Jimmy was that stupid.

After that Kenny Clark let off the Chicken Vicky for a while and started in calling Jimmy the "playboy with the bunny."

Finally Jane looked at her watch and said, "Hey, it's ten-thirty already. We better go meet your father."

"Boy," Judy said, "the time sure went fast. Except for when I was nauseous."

"That Ferris wheel was something," Spider said, smiling happily as if she was reliving the ride. "You really shouldn't have been afraid, Vicky. They're very safe. Maybe if you started out on one of the littler rides. . . ."

At the entrance gate, my father was waiting for us. My mother was with him, grinning broadly, and holding a huge purple plush dog that looked like mine, except it was about ten times bigger.

"Hey!" I said. "I didn't know you were around here. Where'd you get that?"

"I brought your mother back," my father said, "because I couldn't remember the last time I'd been to a carnival myself. Fun, isn't it?"

"Did you win that for Mrs. Benneker?" Spider asked.

"No, Mrs. Benneker won that for herself," my father said. "You know where they give you this big hammer and you have to hit this thing and ring the bell, to test your strength?"

"You did that?" Judy said, staring at my mother.

"She certainly did," my father said. "Look at the muscles on that woman."

My mother, who is very thin and hasn't a muscle to speak of, just smiled sweetly.

"It has nothing to do with muscles," she said. "It's all in your wrists. Just a matter of the right angle of striking. Anyone can do it, if you know how to swing the hammer."

"Wow," Judy said, impressed.

"I said the same thing myself," my father remarked.

We all talked at the same time on the way home, telling my parents about the carnival.

Judy was the first one to be dropped off.

"Hey!" she remembered, as she climbed out of the back seat. "We didn't decide about Halloween yet."

"Here we go again," sighed Jane.

"What are you going to do, Vic?" Judy asked.

I shrugged. "I don't know."

The costume, that was really the problem. What kind of costume could I make by myself that I wouldn't look stupid in? I mean, I couldn't very well go to the store and buy myself a devil suit, because I was too big to fit in the store costumes. And I didn't wear pajamas with feet, so I certainly could not be a bunny rabbit like Lyn Lombardi's brother, even if I wanted to. In fact, the only thing I could think of at the moment was the Ferris wheel, and that made me think that the most appropriate thing I could do was make myself some feathers and wings and go as a big chicken.

"No," I decided finally. "I guess I'm not going out."

I saw my mother and father look at each other. My mother gave a little sigh.

"Then I won't go either," Jane said. "It's too much trouble."

"All that candy and stuff, though," Judy said dreamily.

"It would just make you nauseous," Spider told her.

"Good-bye, childhood," my father murmured as we drove away from Judy's house.

Jane and I looked at each other and shrugged.

Spider smoothed her hair behind her ear and said, "You really missed a great Ferris wheel, Vicky."

I tried to picture her hair dyed bright green.

A definite improvement, I thought.

# V

THE ANNOUNCEMENT came over the PA system one Monday morning:

"All boys and girls who wish to try out for the sixth-grade play should come to the auditorium tomorrow afternoon after dismissal."

"Well," said Mrs. Friedman, "I hope I'll see some of you up there onstage. I know we have lots of budding talent in this class."

Sharon Webb stroked her hair and tried to look modest.

She failed.

Should I try out? I really wanted to. I could almost picture myself onstage, the audience applauding, the lights, the makeup, the excitement of opening night . . . I could see the mimeographed program: STARRING VICTORY BENNEKER! There I was, the star. A little girl climbing up to the stage and handing me a basket of flowers. More flowers, people surrounding me with bouquets. A talent scout from Hollywood: "Miss Benneker, you're just what we've been looking for. I have a contract right here. . . ."

When I got home, my mother was sitting in the middle of the living room floor surrounded by cardboard circles.

"Don't ask," she warned. "Just don't ask."

"Okay," I shrugged, on my way to the kitchen. I knew she was waiting for me to say, "Why are you sitting in the middle of the floor with all those cardboard circles around you?" but I figured she'd tell me quicker if I pretended not to be interested. That's psychology. She uses it on me.

"I am making clocks," she said, following me into the kitchen. "I have just cut out twenty-one cardboard clocks. My class is going to learn to tell time, or else."

I took some milk out of the refrigerator.

"My cutting hand is killing me," she said, rubbing her wrist.

"I'll help," I offered.

"Good." She handed me a Magic Marker. "When you're finished with your milk, you can do the clock faces. Just make the numbers on the circles."

"We have tryouts for the sixth-grade play tomorrow," I said, putting my glass into the sink.

"Oh, really? What kind of a play will it be?"

"I don't know yet. Miss Lang is in charge of it. She wrote the play herself."

"Are you going to try out?"

"I thought I might go tomorrow and see."

55

"Good idea. You could be very talented, I bet."

"I could? How do you know?"

"Why, when you were just five years old, you did the most incredible imitation of Uncle Arnold . . ." She giggled. "Honestly, the whole family used to get hysterical. Except Uncle Arnold, of course."

"Well, if there's an Uncle Arnold in the play, I guess I'm all set."

When my father heard about the play, he was immediately convinced that I was destined to carry on the family acting tradition.

"What family acting tradition?" I asked.

"Well, you know, when I was in college, I was in all the big plays."

"Really? I didn't know about that."

"Oh, yes. As a matter of fact, I even toyed with the idea of making acting my career."

"What stopped you?" I asked, excited at the thought that I might have been the daughter of a famous actor.

"She did," he said, pointing at my mother. "She whispered those four little words in my ear and ruined my hopes for a life on the stage."

"What did you say?" I asked my mother.

"I said," she grinned, " 'You have no talent.' "

The next afternoon, Jane and I went down to the auditorium. As we walked in the door, Miss Lang handed us each a thick sheaf of mimeographed paper. It was the script of her play.

We sat down and looked at it.

*The Pollution Solution* by Elinore Lang.

"That's a catchy title," I remarked.

The auditorium was beginning to fill up and get noisy. Spider and Judy came in and sat down two aisles over.

"Look at this!" said Jane, pointing to the script.

"Characters: Clean Air. Clean Water. Industrial Waste. Smog. Litter. Beer Cans. Good grief."

"Good-bye," I said, standing up. I didn't think I wanted to be in this play at all.

Kenny Clark and Jimmy Fallon slipped into the row behind us.

"Sit down, you're blocking the view," said Kenny, and pressed my shoulder down so hard that I flopped back into my seat.

"This is weird," Jane frowned. "She wrote the whole thing in rhyme."

"I am leaving," I announced. "This is ridiculous. How in the world do you act like Industrial Waste?"

"Talk dirty," Kenny hissed in my ear. He broke himself up.

"*All right, everyone! Attention, please!*" Miss Lang was standing on the stage, clapping her hands to get our attention. The microphone wasn't turned on, so it took a while.

"I guess I'm stuck," I said, slumping back in my seat.

"You don't have to try out," said Jane.

I looked at the script again. Clean Air seemed to be the star.

"Well . . ." I hesitated. I could still picture myself onstage, and I could still hear the cheers of the audience. It was hard to turn your back on a family tradition, I thought, remembering what my father had said.

I tried out for the role of Clean Air.

"Now just read this part here," Miss Lang said, pointing out the lines.

I cleared my throat and stood up very straight. Everyone was watching me.

But you have to get used to that if you're going to be a star, I told myself. You can't be famous if you're going to be afraid of people watching you being famous.

"*I am clean air —*"

"Louder please!" Miss Lang bellowed. "We want to hear you in the back of the auditorium!"

How can you act and scream at the same time, I wondered. Oh, well, maybe you have to learn to scream first, and learning to act comes later.

*"I am clean air, my oxygen flowing*
*"Through your bloodstream will keep you glow-*
     *ing.*
*"For healthy body and level head*
*"You need clean air, or you'll be —"*

"Thank you," Miss Lang called. "Next please."
I went back to my seat.

"I'd rather be a beer can," I grumbled. Jane nodded sympathetically.

Spider got the part of Clean Air. She deserved it. As a matter of fact, she and the play deserved each other.

Jane tried out for Clean Water. I thought she was very good, under the circumstances.

> *"I am water, pure and clear,*
> *"When you drink me you'll have no fear,*
> *"Of detergent foam or slime,*
> *"Industrial waste or grit and grime."*

Behind me, Kenny Clark made himself burp.

Jimmy Fallon got the part of Clean Water. Miss Lang decided that since Clean Air was a girl, Clean Water should be a boy. I don't think anyone but Miss Lang understood why that should be, but it was her play.

I tried out for the part of Smog, too. I thought I'd

like to try being a nasty villain, since everyone really remembers the villain in a play.

I tried to scream in a very hideous voice:

> *"Breathe me, breathe me, breathe me in!*
> *"Your suffering is about to begin!*
> *"I sting your eyes and stuff your nose,*
> *"I clog your lungs and ruin your clothes!"*

From trying to scream so they could hear me in the back of the auditorium, and trying to sound hideous at the same time, I strained my voice so that I began to cough uncontrollably. Everyone thought that was very funny, except Miss Lang. I think maybe she was very sensitive about her play.

"Thank you," she said coldly. "Next."

I didn't get the part of Smog.

After all the main parts were filled, Miss Lang asked everyone else who still wanted to be in the play to come up front. I wasn't going to, but Jane dragged me along with her.

"We have to rehearse almost every day," she whispered, "and you get to be excused from class. Come on."

Miss Lang divided us into three groups. "Beer Cans and Soda Bottles," she said, pointing at Jane's group. "Industrial Waste," she said, pointing at the second group. "Litter," she said, pointing at my group.

"Now go home and read the script. Familiarize yourselves with your parts. You'll have to start memorizing them right away. I'll see you all on Thursday at two."

"What's to memorize?" I shrugged, walking out of the auditorium with Jane.

"Well, it's a start, anyway," Jane said.

"What do you mean?"

"You know, all actresses have to start somewhere. They don't just happen to be stars. They get very small parts, and struggle and starve until somebody finally discovers them."

"Spider's starting out being a star. She didn't have to struggle and starve."

"Miss Lang only picked her," Jane said firmly, "because she looks clean. It's what you call typecasting. Sharon looks like Clean Air."

I tried to picture Spider in rags, her face dirty, and her hair covered with dead leaves. She comes to my house, begging for a piece of stale bread and a glass of water. I throw her a dollar and slam the door before she can kiss my hand in gratitude.

I got home kind of late because we had to walk. My mother was in the kitchen, cutting arrows out of black construction paper.

"How was the audition?" she asked, as soon as I walked in.

"Okay," I shrugged.

"Did you get a part?"

"Well, sort of."

"What are you?"

"Litter."

"Litter?" she repeated, stopping in the middle of an arrow.

"Want to see the script?" I asked.

She held out her hand and I gave her the script.

"The Pollution Solution. By Elinore Lang. Characters: Clean Air. Clean Water. Smog. Industrial Waste. Litter — oh, there you are."

"Yeah. I guess I don't have as much acting talent as you thought."

"Oh, I wouldn't say that," she disagreed. "Just because you didn't get the starring role this time —"

"Let's face it," I said, sitting down at the table. "I take after my father."

"Well," she grinned, "that isn't so bad, either."

"What are you doing now?" I asked.

"These are the hands for those clocks," she said. "How about helping me?"

"Sure. What should I do?"

"Get another pair of scissors and you can do the big hands while I do the little hands."

I used a cardboard stencil to draw the form on the construction paper, then I cut out the arrows. It was boring work; after the first couple of times you didn't even have to think about what you were doing.

My mother turned on the radio.

"There's no business like show business . . ." some group was singing. "Like no business I know! . . . Ev'rything about it is appealing . . ."

"Ladies and gentlemen, we're here in the lobby of the Santa Monica Auditorium, and we're going to try and see if we can talk to any of the stars on their way inside. It's the greatest night of the year here in Hollywood, Academy Award night, when the movie industry honors its most talented members.

"I hear the crowd screaming outside, somebody just pulled up in a silver Cadillac, I can't see who it is yet, but the fans outside are going wild! Can you hear them? I'll bet they can hear them screaming even inside the auditorium!

"Oh, there she is! No wonder, folks, it's *Victory Benneker!* Look, she's coming this way, she's coming in, *here she comes!*

"Miss Benneker, Miss Benneker, will you say a word to our television audience? Please, Miss Benneker?"

"My goodness!" Victory laughed breathlessly. "That's quite a crowd out there!"

"And they do love you, don't they?" beamed the announcer.

"I hope so," Victory said modestly, "because I certainly love them."

"Miss Benneker, everyone is saying you're sure to win the Oscar for Best Actress tonight. What do you think about that?"

"Well, I hope everyone is right," Victory smiled. "It would be a great honor. But the competition is really stiff this year."

"Good luck, Miss Benneker!"

"Thank you."

Inside the auditorium almost every seat was filled. Television cameras scanned the audience for famous stars, and spotlights shone on celebrities as the cameras found them.

Victory Benneker, Hollywood's newest and brightest star, took her seat as the TV cameras focused on her, and the bright light lit up her now-famous smile.

Dozens of awards had to be handed out. It seemed like an eternity before the Best Actor and Best Actress awards were ready to be presented. But finally. . . .

"And now, ladies and gentlemen, the moment we've all been waiting for. The nominees for Best Actress are: Laura Marlow in *Blue Wednesday* . . ."

There was applause and cheers for all the nominees. But when Biff Seeger, the emcee, read, "Victory Benneker, for *Pure as the Air I Breathe*," the audience went wild. The television camera turned on Victory; she smiled modestly and lowered her eyes. If the suspense was unbearable, she was not showing it. But, then, she was an *actress*.

"The envelope, please. And the winner is . . . *Victory Benneker!*"

The cheers of the audience seemed to lift her to her feet. As if she could hardly believe it, she worked her way slowly to the front of the auditorium, and up onto the stage. She was not acting now, no doubt about it. Her eyes were filled with real tears, as Biff Seeger handed her the golden statuette.

"I don't know what to say," she murmured into the microphone. "I really don't know what to say. If you could hear the way my heart is beating, I wouldn't have to say anything!"

The audience laughed appreciatively.

"There are so many people I ought to thank: my director, the wonderful actors I worked with in the picture, the Academy for bestowing this great honor upon me. But most of all, I guess I ought to thank my father — because I take after him."

Victory hugged her Oscar and walked off stage. The applause was deafening. . . .

"Anybody home?"

"We're in the kitchen," my mother answered.

"Hi," my father said. "How did the tryouts for the play go?"

"I take after you," I sighed.

"That's wonderful!" my father said happily.

# VI

REHEARSALS for the sixth-grade play were held almost every afternoon after lunch and I got absolutely no satisfaction out of getting off that period. As a matter of fact, I was pretty mad at Jane for having forced me into the play at all, since the only thing we ever missed was gym twice a week, and while I'm not crazy about gym, it isn't like getting out of math or something. The days there was no gym, the kids in the class did whatever they wanted, because there were eleven of us in the play from our class, and Mrs. Friedman figured she didn't want to do anything important while half the class was gone.

And boring — wow. When you get right down to it, Litter is not a very interesting part to play. I mean, all I did was lie there on the stage. Toward the end of the play, Kenny Clark, who was the Park Sanitation Attendant, came along and swept me up along with the other Litter. Then I rolled off stage as he prodded me with a broom.

My mother was not happy about my part in the play at all. The stage was not swept very often, and I would get covered with dust and dirt during every rehearsal.

"Look at you!" my mother shrieked, the first day I came home after rehearsing. "What happened?"

"We practiced the play today."

"But you're Litter, not Garbage. I thought you were going to be a nice clean newspaper or something like that."

"I am, but I have to lie down on the stage. That's how I got dirty."

"Good God, it seems to me Miss Lang ought to get her own environment cleaned up a little while she's taking care of pollution. Well, you'll just have to wear jeans to school on the days you have rehearsals."

"Yay!"

Another thing my mother didn't like too much was that I was always practicing at home. Not that there was anything much to practice. But she and my father tripped over me a lot as I lay on the floor doing nothing, just thinking, "I am Litter." And rolling out of the room once in a while.

I guess maybe I thought I'd feel more like a dedicated actress if I practiced even when I didn't have to. Also, I could put off doing homework and things by rehearsing. And my father could see that I was really serious about the family acting tradition, even if I did only have a little part with nothing to say.

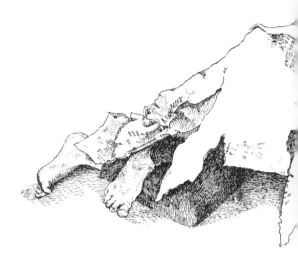

"I'll tell you this," he said to my mother one night. "No one is going to say she didn't know her part."

"Yes," my mother agreed, "she certainly is getting good at it, isn't she? She can lie there like that for hours at a time."

Well, that wasn't really true. I rolled away sometimes. And every once in a while, I would flap my arms a little bit, as if a breeze had come up and I was fluttering. I thought it added a little character to the part.

Miss Lang was not too excited about that, though.

"What are you doing? You there, Litter, why are you moving around like that?"

I lifted my head to look at her.

"A wind came up," I explained. "I'm blowing around."

"Well, please, just do what I told you to. I don't want you blowing around. It's very distracting. Now it's not so hard just to lie there, is it?"

"No," I sighed. But it's very *boring*, I said to myself. And my arms fall asleep.

"Then please follow my directions."

After what felt like hundreds of rehearsals, the week of the play finally came. Miss Lang told us we would have a dress rehearsal Wednesday morning, and present the play for the whole school and our parents on Thursday morning.

My mother and I had made my costume out of five sheets of the *New York Times*, and they had to be pinned on over my clothes. I didn't know how I was going to get it on without my mother helping me, but on Wednesday morning I took a box of safety pins and my newspapers and went straight to the auditorium.

Jane was a beer can, and her costume was easy to get on, because she just slipped it over her head.

"That's terrific," I said admiringly. "How did you make it?"

"My father did it. My mother said it cost a dollar seventy-nine just for aluminum foil."

"Listen, I don't know how I'm going to get these newspapers on."

"Here, I'll do the back for you," Janey offered. "I'll pin it to your sweater."

The newspapers tore a little bit as Jane pinned them on my shoulders, but I didn't think it would matter. Litter is supposed to be messy anyhow.

Dress rehearsal didn't go too well. Miss Lang screamed a lot; one of the soda bottles ripped his costume, which was made of green Saran Wrap, and Smog forgot his lines three times.

"Well, I'm sure you'll all be just wonderful tomorrow," Miss Lang said weakly, at the end of rehearsal. She didn't sound as if she believed it at all. What she sounded like, really, was like she was going to cry.

"You know, I'm getting a little nervous," I said to my mother that afternoon. "Isn't that stupid?"

"Not at all," she said. "It's perfectly natural. You wouldn't be normal if you didn't get nervous."

"But I don't have a big part or anything."

"You don't have to be the star to get a little touch of stage fright."

"Is that what I've got?" I asked, surprised.

"I think so. But it always disappears when you get on stage. You know the best thing to do the day before a play?"

"Rehearse a lot?" I guessed.

"Oh, no, just the opposite. Professional actors forget all about the play and their parts. They go out and do something that takes their minds off being nervous."

Which is why, when Jane called and asked me to go ice skating — because her mother told her that professional actors always forget all about the play the day before opening night — I said okay.

Ordinarily I'd have said no, because I am even worse at ice skating than I am at dancing. It must be my coordination or weak ankles or something like that, I don't know exactly what. But every time I try to skate, I fall. Sometimes I fall *before* I even try.

But I figured, if this is what actors do before a play, I guess I ought to do it. Nothing would take my mind off the play like falling down and breaking my legs.

Jane called for me because my house is on the way to the park. She was wearing a short red skating skirt and a white sweater and she had her ice skates with red tassels swung over her shoulder.

I wore a pair of old jeans. My mother wouldn't buy me a skating skirt because she said it was ridiculous to buy a skating skirt for someone who hated to skate. I didn't have ice skates either. I had to rent them at the park, because when she did buy me ice skates one year, I used them exactly once before my feet grew two sizes, and she said that was a ridiculous waste of money too. The skates at the park didn't have red tassels.

The park was crowded when we got there; it was the first really cold day of December, and the rink had only been opened for the season the week before.

"Look at all those people," I said nervously, clumping out from the skate rental booth. My ankles caved in, and I would have fallen down if Jane hadn't grabbed my arm.

"I wish they made double runner skates in my size," I grumbled, wobbling toward the rink.

"You don't need double runners," Jane said sternly. "You just need practice. How do you expect to be able to skate if you never try?"

"I don't expect to be able to skate even if I *do* try."

"You want to skate with me?" Jane asked as she started out onto the ice.

"No, you'd better let me hold onto the rail for a while. I have to get my balance."

"You'll never get your balance hanging onto the rail," she said disapprovingly, and skated away.

I inched around the side of the rink, clinging to the railing for support. I made very bad time, because the ice was so crowded. It must have taken me fifteen minutes just to go halfway around.

Over on the other side of the rink, there was some-one else hanging onto the railing too. Well, I told my-self, I'm not the only person in the world who can't skate. As I worked my way around to the other side, I could see that it was a teen-age boy wearing a blue sweat shirt with white lettering on it. I couldn't see what the letters said, but he made me feel pretty good.

I mean, if a teen-age boy, in the best of health, with a rugged athletic look to him wasn't ashamed of hang-ing onto the rail and showing the world he was no ice skater, why should I be?

I began to feel a little more confident, and I actu-ally let go of the rail as I came near him and struck out with my right foot gliding smoothly, as Jane had showed me.

I took one beautiful, perfect stroke. Then I brought my left foot forward for the second stroke — and kicked myself in the back of my right foot, tripped over my own skates, and fell flat on my face.

I skidded along the ice on my stomach and landed right at the feet of the boy in the blue sweat shirt.

"Are you all right?" he asked, bending over me.

I struggled to stand up. He put out a hand to help me, but I staggered and began to slip again.

I'll pull us both down, I thought wildly. I'll drag us both, screaming, to our deaths.

But he grabbed my arms and lifted me to my feet

and I wondered how such a lousy skater could have such good balance that he could keep us both from sprawling all over the ice and getting maimed, or worse.

"Would you like some help getting around?" he said.

From you? I thought.

I brushed the hair and the tears out of my eyes and looked at his sweat shirt. The lettering said, "Long Island Parks Dep't."

He was a rink attendant. He was not a lousy skater at all, it was his *job* to stand at the side of the rink and pick up people like me when they fall down, and take little kids around the ice once or twice and make sure none of the boys grab people's scarves and try to choke them.

"You want to go around? I'll take you."

"Sure, okay," I said. It was better than hanging onto the rail, and he wouldn't let me fall.

He held our hands in front of us and said, "Now just keep moving — move your feet whenever you feel like it."

He started off and pulled me along. He was right — I didn't have to do a thing. His movement kept us both gliding smoothly across the ice.

Suddenly I felt as if I could really skate. The music they were playing over the loudspeaker seemed to be right in time to our rhythm. I forgot all about the other skaters; it was like I was the only one who could skate, and they were all standing around, admiring me and gasping in amazement as I swirled around the ice.

I forgot I was wearing old dungarees and rented skates. I forgot that I was skating with the rink attendant, and that if he let me go I would fall down and crack my ribs. I forgot everything, except the feel of the wind blowing my scarf out behind me, and the cold air stinging my face. . . .

"All right, ladies and gentlemen, Victory Benneker is halfway through her free-skating program here at the Winter Olympics, and so far, she's been absolutely perfect. Not one mistake; the little girl from Oakvale, Long Island, has the spectators here holding their breath.

"But she has a couple of really difficult moves coming up, first a double axel, then a triple lutz, and then right into another double axel. A very tough series of jumps, very tough.

"If she does that triple lutz, she'll be the first American woman to do it successfully in Olympic competition. Here it comes, here it comes! The double axel — perfect! Now the triple — *she did it, she did it!* And right into the double — *perfect, perfect!*

"Ladies and gentlemen, this crowd is rising to its feet, you can see them on your television screens, you can hear the cheers! There's the end of her performance, and the little girl from Oakvale has this audience of seasoned Olympic spectators absolutely screaming!

"And now the judges are ready with her marks. Remember, six is the perfect score, and she needs five-point-eights and five-point-nines to beat out Ingrid Schmidt of West Germany for the gold medal. Here come the marks!

"Six! Six! This is incredible! She has two — no, three — no, she has *all sixes!* Ladies and gentlemen, in all my years of sports reporting, I've never seen anything like this before!

"She has all sixes! *Every single judge has given Victory Benneker a perfect mark of six! This is incredible, incredible, what an unbelievable performance, what a skater, I can't believe it, the crowd is going wild!"*

"Here we are. Think you can manage on your own now?"

I looked around. We were back at the rail again, back at the skating rink. I was not wearing a silver skating skirt with sequins, but my old jeans, and the boy was going off to help someone else.

The crowd was not cheering me. Anyone who

wasn't skating was watching a tiny kid, about six years old, in the middle of the ice; she was wearing a little green skirt and a white sweater, and no one was holding her hand.

She skated around, doing figure eights and gliding on one skate, and gracefully arching her arms over her head as she practiced spinning.

A woman behind me said to her friend, "Look at that little girl! She can't be more than six. Isn't she incredible?"

"Six? Six? I don't believe it!"

"I know. She really is amazing."

Little show-off.

The sixth-grade play was not a total disaster *just* because of me. By the time I loused up my part, *The Pollution Solution* was already well on its way to becoming the worst show ever put on by any elementary school in the history of the United States.

First of all, the audience laughed at all the serious parts. Miss Lang didn't like that at all.

Smog forgot almost all of his lines, and most of the time just stood there and looked dirty. He had a very strange costume made of some filmy gray kind of material, and half the kids thought he was Tinkerbelle.

There were a lot of parents in the audience too, including mine, and they kept laughing in the wrong places also, and the teachers couldn't do anything to make *them* behave.

Well, by the time it got to the part where the Litter is swept up by Kenny Clark with his giant broom, I was not only embarrassed, bored, and wishing I'd been sick and stayed home, but my whole body was asleep.

You know how, when your foot's asleep, you can't move it at all, you can't even feel it?

Well, my *whole body* was asleep, not just my foot. I was completely numb, from the neck down, and when Kenny came along and prodded me with his broom, meaning I was supposed to start rolling off stage with the rest of the Litter, I couldn't move at all. Not at all.

So Kenny, thinking my head must have been asleep too, repeated his lines:

*"Now I'll sweep till the park is clean,*
*"So children can play where it's pretty and green!"*

And he jabbed me with his broom, right in the ribs, which were still sore from falling on the ice the day before.

"*Yow!*" I yelled.

The audience screamed with laughter.

"Move, stupid!" Kenny hissed, poking me with his broom.

I began to roll, slowly, painfully, offstage.

All five sheets of my *New York Times* costume ripped as the curtain came down.

But I don't think Miss Lang was crying only because of me.

# VII

E VERYBODY," I said to my mother one gloomy Saturday, "*everybody* has seen *Eye of the Snake* except me."

"What a tragedy," clucked my mother, not even looking up from her book. "I hope you aren't marked for life."

My mother does not like to be interrupted when she's reading.

"Can Jane and I go this afternoon?"

"I thought," said my mother, putting a finger in her book to mark the place, "that you were the only person in the world who hasn't seen it."

"All right," I sighed, "so we're the only two people. Can I? It's rated 'PG.' "

"Meaning 'putrid and gory,' " my father remarked.

"It does not! It means 'children of all ages admitted, parental guidance — ' "

"I know, I know," said my father. "Sometimes I think you're losing your sense of humor."

"Why is it impossible to get a straight answer from anybody in this house!" I wailed.

"Go!" said my mother, pointing toward the door. "There's a straight answer. Go!"

"Thank you," I sighed gratefully.

"And if there's any cursing, hold your hands over your ears," my father suggested.

"Good grief," I replied.

Jane's father drove us to the movies.

"My mother says *Eye of the Snake* is a disgusting title. She shivers every time I say it," Jane remarked, as we drove through the rain.

"Well, your mother has a thing about snakes. My father says 'PG' stands for 'putrid and gory.'"

"That's funny. My mother says it stands for 'portrayed grossly.'"

"What does that mean?" I asked.

"That means rotten," explained Mr. Marshall.

When we got to the theater we had just enough time to buy popcorn and Milk Duds and two boxes of Good 'n' Plenty before the cartoons.

There weren't too many people there. The movie had been held over two weeks in a row, so I guess almost everybody *had* seen it already.

It was about this scientist, Dr. Framingham, who had invented a new weapon so powerful and so terrifying that all the big countries sent spies to get the weapon before any other country could get it. And to try and kill off all the other spies who were after the weapon.

The British spy was a woman who wore shorts and leather boots all the time, and at the end, she and the American spy are the only ones left alive. They fall in love, but you're not sure whether they really trust each other or not, because after all, they're spies and you never know. The ending was kind of vague, but they're either going to get married, or kill each other.

"Wasn't that a great movie," sighed Jane as we walked into the lobby.

"Yeah. I wonder how you get to be a spy?"

We waited outside for Jane's father, who was going to pick us up.

"I don't know," Jane said, "but I'll bet it isn't easy. Can you withstand torture?"

"What?"

"Well, what if you were a spy, and you had some very important information that the other side wanted? How do you think they'd try and get it?"

"Oh. I see what you mean."

I thought about it for a moment.

"I don't know," I finally admitted. "I've never actually been tortured."

"Well, you see, they'd have to have someone who could withstand torture. And you have to be very clever and sneaky. Like when Vera was locked in that cabin on the mountain with the vicious guard dog outside. . . . They probably give you an aptitude test to see if you're a fast thinker."

"I guess so," I agreed.

Mr. Marshall pulled up in front of the theater.

As we got in the car, Jane continued, "And also, you have to have impeccable credentials. They'd run a security check on you first thing."

"Well, I've never been arrested," I said.

"Glad to hear it," muttered Mr. Marshall.


When I got home, my father and mother were standing on the living room sofa hanging a picture.

"Why did you take the other picture down?" I asked.

"So we could hang this one," my mother explained. She sounded annoyed.

"But isn't this the one Aunt Clara gave you? I thought you didn't like it."

"We like it," my father said shortly.

"How come you like it now?" I persisted. It was a picture of a boy and a dog. They both had big eyes. They were smelling a flower. No dog I ever heard of smelled flowers.

"Because Aunt Clara's coming," my mother snapped.

"That's dishonest! You shouldn't pretend you like it if you really don't."

"Look," my father said patiently, "you wouldn't want to hurt someone's feelings, would you?"

"Well, no," I admitted.

"So while she's here, we'll just make her happy by letting her see we appreciate her gift."

"Okay," I shrugged. "Suit yourself. I just hope she doesn't think we love it so much that she decides to give us another painting."

My parents looked at each other. Their eyes seemed to get almost as big as the boy's and the dog's. Without another word, my father took the picture off the wall, and my mother handed him our own picture to put back up again. Then he carried Aunt Clara's picture back down to the basement.

"Well," said my mother, stepping down off the couch. "How did you like the movie?"

"It was really good," I said. "It was about spies. See, there was this Dr. Fram —"

"Listen," my father cut in, coming back up the stairs, "I'm going to have to pick Clara up at the station pretty soon. If you want me to get anything from the store, you'd better make me a list."

"Oh, Lord, what is she allowed to eat? I never can remember," my mother said frantically, rummaging through a drawer for a pencil and paper. "I wish she'd give us a little more warning instead of dropping in like this."

"I think she's allergic to tomatoes," my father said, wrinkling up his forehead in concentration. "And she has to watch her cholesterol —"

"And nothing spicy," my mother remembered, "and no salt — oh, we'd better have fish."

"Blechh," I muttered, going up to my room.

I looked out the window. It was raining harder now. I wished I had gone home with Jane. Aunt Clara could be a real pain in the neck. She always felt my parents weren't doing enough to bring out my "potential," and that I could really be talented at something if only she could find something I was talented *at*.

So she brought me things that were supposed to inspire me to be creative. Like, last time she brought me a wooden flute and thought I ought to be able to play folk songs on it. She was very disappointed when I couldn't even figure out how to find the notes to "Mary Had a Little Lamb."

I looked out the window. My father was hurrying to the car, hunched up in his raincoat. It was dark out, almost like it was six o'clock instead of four. I could hear my mother in the kitchen, banging drawers shut and rattling pots and pans.

The rain was driving against my window, beating

so hard on the glass that it almost drowned out the
sounds coming from downstairs. . . .

"Beastly weather we're having," said the man behind the lead-lined desk. He looked at Victory's shorts
and leather boots.

"Don't you get chilly dressed that way?"

"Oh, no," she said lightly. "I'm completely impervious to heat and cold. I've trained myself. Just a matter of concentration."

"Amazing. Now, Miss Benneker, I know you're anxious to learn the results of your aptitude tests."

"I hope I did well," Victory said a little nervously. "I'm really looking foward to being a spy."

"Well, now, we don't call ourselves spies, you know. We're known as agents."

"Oh, excuse me."

"Perfectly all right. Now, on your aptitude tests your scores were among the highest ever achieved in the history of our agency. It is not our policy to reveal actual scores, but confidentially," he lowered his voice, "it is impossible to score higher than you did."

"Thank you."

"Your security clearance went through without a hitch. Your credentials are impeccable. Your physical examination showed no handicaps, chronic illnesses or malfunctions. In other words, you are a perfect physical specimen and in the very best of condition."

"I try to take care of myself," she nodded.

"I guess that all there's left for me to say is, 'Welcome to the Agency.' Glad to have you aboard."

He shook her hand warmly.

"Now, Miss Benneker, for your first assignment. Can you be ready to fly to Paris tonight?"

Victory gasped. So soon! She'd expected a day or so to say good-bye to her family and to write her will. But —

"Yes, I'll be ready."

"Good. Now, somewhere in the Louvre museum a formula is hidden. It was hidden by Dr. Winston, just before he was captured by enemy agents. *We have got to get that formula!* It is vital to national security that we know the formula before the enemy can get it out of Dr. Winston — if he's still alive. Do you understand?"

"Yes."

"It could be anywhere. All we know is that a guard saw him taken off by two men from the Louvre, and we're sure he hid the formula before he was captured. Your flight will leave Kennedy Airport at midnight. Be careful, and good luck."

"Thank you, Mr. — er —"

" 'Q.' You will know me only as 'Q.' "

"Thank you, Q."


Paris — City of Lights — was completely dark when she broke into the Louvre museum. It was as if the driving rain had put out a million candles, leaving everything in blackness.

There are over five thousand paintings in the Louvre, not to mention statues, sculpture, objets d'art, etc., and once she'd deactivated the alarm system with her deactivating equipment provided by Q and picked the burglar-proof locks, Victory saw right away that she wasn't going to have time to stand around and admire anything.

The formula could be any place — behind any painting, beneath any small piece of sculpture — even flushed down the toilet in the men's room, for all she knew — if Dr. Winston had had time to do that before he was captured.

Well, there wasn't anything she could do about that last possibility, but she certainly didn't want to waste time worrying about it.

She started down the first corridor.

Her pencil-thin flashlight illuminated only a small area at a time, but she had trained herself to see almost perfectly in the dark, so she only needed it to examine the backs of canvases. Victory proceeded systematically, going over each picture as she came to it, feeling around the frame and behind it, even running her hand against the wall it was hanging on.

Suddenly, her fingers tingled. Behind a huge painting in a massive gilt frame, she felt a piece of thin paper and a wad of chewing gum. Good thinking, Dr. Winston! She shined her flashlight on the spot, holding the heavy picture away from the wall with one hand.

Sure enough, figures, numbers, strange symbols were scrawled all over the paper.

What luck! She'd found the formula already!

Carefully, very carefully, Victory began to pull at the gum, trying to unstick it from the back of the picture. It was hard working with one hand, and her other arm was beginning to grow numb from the effort of holding the picture out from the wall.

Suddenly she was blinded by a circle of light, and a voice barked, "Don't move!"

She dropped the edge of the picture and it slammed back against the wall, the chewing gum and the formula still attached.

"Well, well, what have we got here? Find anything interesting?"

Victory couldn't see a thing, because they were shining their light directly into her eyes. She tried to shield her face with one hand, but it did no good.

"Who are you?" she demanded. "What are you doing here?"

"Well, my dear, we might ask you the same thing — but we already know what you're doing here. Have you found it?"

"I don't know what you're talking about," she snapped.

"So, you're merely sight-seeing, eh? Kind of an odd hour to be strolling through the Louvre." His voice got hard and ugly. "All right now, let's stop kidding each other, Miss Benneker. We know why you're here and we want to know what you've found. There are ways to make you talk, you know."

"I might as well inform you," she said coldly, "I can withstand torture."

He laughed an ugly laugh.

"Who said anything about torture? You Americans see too many movies. Have you ever heard of sodium pentothal?"

"Truth serum!" She gasped. Victory had never trained herself to withstand truth serum. She couldn't let them capture her — not while she knew where the formula was hidden.

"All right, Max, let's go."

Two of them!

Instantly she was grabbed from behind, a hairy arm across her throat. She kicked her foot out behind her, flung her body forward, and with a bloodcurdling shriek which she had mastered during her karate lessons Victory tossed her attacker over her shoulder to the floor.

"Okay, kid, you wanna play games? Get her, Moose!"

Three of them! But they couldn't kill her — not if they wanted to find out where Dr. Winston's formula was.

Heavy footsteps thudded toward her. The man he called Moose must be enormous! Victory steeled herself for a battle. Should she scream? No — spies don't scream, she told herself firmly. But they can back away, she thought, backing away till she felt her shoulders touch the wall behind her. A huge hand gripped her neck and she —

"Victory!" my mother called in a sugary voice, not at all like her real voice. "Aunt Clara's here."

I was back in my room. The same rain was slanting against the same window, and it was the same old me. Every dreary thing was the same, except that now, with Aunt Clara here, things would be a little drearier.

"I'm coming," I sighed.

"I called you three times," my mother chided sweetly as I dragged downstairs.

"Hello, dear!" Aunt Clara said brightly, swooping me into her arms for a very lipsticky kiss.

"Look what I've brought you!"

"Oh, thank you, Aunt Clara," I said, trying to sound as grateful as she expected me to be. "I can't wait to see what it is." Well, that much was true.

I tore the wrapping and the ribbon off, as my parents and Aunt Clara hovered over me, waiting for my reaction.

It was a paint-by-numbers kit.

And the picture was of a small girl and a cat, both with very big eyes, both smelling a flower.

# VIII

I WOKE UP on Tuesday morning to hear the wind howling around the house, and I ran to my window. Snow was whipping against the pane, and the entire street was buried under what looked like mountains of snow.

"*Yay!*" I yelled, and ran downstairs.

My mother and father were in the kitchen with the radio on.

"Is this a blizzard?" I yelled. "Would you call this a blizzard?"

"Shh!" My mother turned the radio up. The announcer was reading a list of schools that were closed because of the storm.

"Are we closed? Are we closed?" I demanded.

"*Shh!*"

"The Oakvale Public Schools, District number eighteen —"

"*Yay!*"

"Thank goodness," my mother said, leaning back in her chair. "I can't imagine how I would have gotten to school."

"Don't be silly," my father said, pouring himself another cup of coffee. "Nobody's going any place today. Including me."

I ran to the kitchen window. The whole back yard was white, and drifts had piled up almost to the top of the fence.

"Wow! Look at that!"

"You look at it," my father said unappreciatively. "You don't have to shovel it."

"Neither do you," my mother pointed out, "unless you can find a way to get the garage door open so you can get to the snow shovel."

My father groaned.

"Hey, what'll we do?" I asked. The snow was piled up against the back door. I could see it just by looking through the glass in the storm door. The snow drift was practically up to my waist.

"Pray for a hot spell," my father advised.

The phone rang. My parents stared at it.

"I'll get it," I said.

"I can't believe it's working," my mother marveled.

"Hi Vic — it's me. Did you hear on the radio?"

"Hi Jane — isn't it great? Isn't it beautiful?"

"Yeah, it's a regular blizzard, the weatherman said. Listen, you want to come over?"

"Wait a minute —" I turned to my parents. "Can I go over to Jane's?"

"Are you kidding?" demanded my father.

"Oh, yeah, I forgot." I turned back to the phone. "Hey, we're snowed in. Can you come over here?"

"Nope — we're snowed in too. That's why my mother told me to ask *you*. My father left the snow shovel in the garage, and there's a big drift in front of the garage door."

"My father did too," I began to giggle. "Isn't that funny?"

"Get off the phone!" my father snapped. "I have to make a call."

"I'll call you later," I said hastily, and hung up.

My father glared at me as he took the receiver off the hook again. He waited.

He scowled at the receiver and jiggled the hook.

"I knew it was too good to be true," my mother sighed.

He slammed the phone back down. "What did you do to it?" he growled at me.

"Good grief!" I protested.

My mother made me some breakfast while my father tried in vain to use the phone.

"Oh, forget it," my mother said finally. "Who's going to be in your office to answer it anyhow?"

"I guess you're right," he agreed, and dropped the receiver back on the hook again.

After breakfast I watched television. There was a

show on about this billionaire who decides to give away a million dollars whenever he feels like it, to people he doesn't even know. The mother of a wounded war veteran had just gotten her tax-free million-dollar check when the television picture faded out and the screen went black.

"Hey!" I yelled, twisting the on-off knob back and forth. "Hey, the TV went off!"

"Oh, great," said my mother, "the radio's off too. It must be a power failure."

"Rats," I grumbled. "Why couldn't it at least happen at night, so we could use candles?"

"Don't worry," my father assured me, "if I know the electric company, we'll still be blacked out by the time it gets dark."

"Now I won't find out what that woman does with her million dollars."

"What woman?" asked my mother.

"On television." I told her about the program I had been watching.

"Good Lord," my father exclaimed. "Are they still running that show?"

"And now I'll never know how she spent the money," I repeated.

"Well, use your imagination," my mother suggested. "What would *you* do with a million dollars?"

A million dollars?

What would *I* do with a million dollars?

I wandered back into the living room and flopped down on the couch in front of the silent TV set. A million dollars . . . Well, let me see, now. . . .

"Hey, Vicky, where'd you get the car?"

Jimmy Fallon and Mark Vogel gazed longingly at her red Jaguar convertible.

"Wow, that's some car," Sharon Webb said jealousy.

"Yes, it is, isn't it?" Victory replied.

"Can I have a ride in it?" they all asked at once.

"Sure. But I can only take one at a time. Hop in, Mark, you can go first."

He climbed in next to her.

"When do I get to go?" Spider whined.

"We'll see," Victory said airily, and waved at them as she gunned the accelerator and sped away.

"Okay folks," Victory said to the kids at the Burger Barn. "My treat. Order whatever you want."

"Wow," they gasped, "Vicky sure is generous. Thanks a lot."

"Oh, think nothing of it," she shrugged off their compliments. "When you've got it, spend it, that's my motto."

"Well, you sure are spending it," Spider said. "But where did you get it?"

"Don't be nosy," Victory warned her, "or I won't put any of my fortune in your father's bank."


"Hey, Vicky, is this your new movie house?"

"Yeah, come on in. Everything's free — for my friends."

"Wow — and you're only going to show good movies, it says on the sign."

"Right. Today we're showing *Eye of the Snake.*"

"Yay!"

"And the candy's free, too, and the popcorn. Just tell Janey what you want. She's running the candy counter."

"Hurray for Vicky!"


"Good morning, Mr. Webb," she said, walking into his office at the First National Bank of Oakvale.

"Why, it's Victory Benneker," he said, getting up to greet her. "You're a friend of Sharon's, aren't you?"

"Well, I wouldn't exactly put it that way," she replied.

"What can I do for you?" he asked politely.

"I just thought I ought to tell you," she explained, perching on his desk, "that I've bought your bank."

"You *what!*" he gasped, clutching his throat.

"And you're working for me, now. That is, if I don't fire you."

"Fire me? Why would you want to do that?"

"I don't know," she shrugged. "Your daughter sort of gets on my nerves."

"Frankly," he said, sitting down again heavily, "she gets on my nerves too, sometimes."

"Really? I didn't realize that. Well, I guess you can't help it if she's a rotten kid," Victory said generously. "Don't worry, Mr. Webb. I won't fire you."

"Bless you, Miss Benneker," he whispered humbly.

"That's okay," Victory shrugged.


The sound of shattering glass and my father cursing woke me out of my daydream.

I went into the kitchen. The glass panes had been removed from the aluminum storm door, and propped up against the wall. Only one, however, was propped up against the wall now. There was glass scattered all around my father, who was leaning through the opening in the storm door, trying to brush snow away from the steps with a broom.

"What are you doing?" I asked curiously.

"I am practicing for the Olympic hockey team!" he roared.

"You don't have to be sarcastic," I said reproachfully, reaching out for the refrigerator door.

"Don't open that!" my mother ordered.

"Why not?" I asked, yanking my hand back.

"The food will spoil if you open it too often."

"But I'm hungry. Besides, it's about fifteen degrees out. You could always put the food outside. If we ever *get* outside."

My father stared at me. Angrily.

"If you're hungry, take a cracker," my mother said.

"But I'm not hungry for a cracker," I objected.

"A starving person will eat anything," she insisted.

"But I'm not starving," I said. "I'm just hungry."

"Why," my father demanded softly, "are you deliberately trying to be difficult?"

"Me?" I cried indignantly. "*Me*, being difficult?"

"I hate the winter," my mother murmured to no one in particular. "I hate it."

"Do you?" I said curiously. "I love it."

By lunchtime I really was starving. The electricity still wasn't on, and my mother opened the refrigerator door and grabbed milk, butter and cheese and slammed the door shut quickly.

"You know what I'd like?" I said dreamily. "A melted cheese sandwich and a nice hot cup of cocoa."

"You know what you're getting?" my mother asked. "A plain American cheese sandwich and a nice cold glass of milk. The stove is electric, you know."

"I know," I sighed. "Hey, why can't Daddy use the barbecue? Then we could have soup and grilled cheese sandwiches, and you could have coffee."

"Coffee," my mother murmured lovingly.

"Well, why not?" I demanded. "Isn't that a good idea?"

"It really is," she agreed. "But somehow I don't think your father would like to stand out there in the snow trying to cook on a charcoal grill."

"I could do it," I offered. "I know how. I've been watching you all do it for years."

"No," she said firmly. "We'll wait for the electricity to come back on."

"You know what this family doesn't have?" I said in disgust.

"What?" my mother asked.

"This family doesn't have any imagination."

"I suppose you're right," my mother admitted.


It got very boring during the afternoon. No TV, no records, the batteries for the transistor radio were dead, and nothing to eat — nothing very good, any-how — *and* I'd finished all my library books.

I shoveled snow for a while, after my father dug out the snow shovel, and that got me so tired and cold that I didn't even want to stay out and try to make a snow-man.

Finally, at four-thirty, just as my mother was hunting around the house for candles, the electricity came back on.

"Thank goodness," she said in relief. "I honestly don't think we have a candle in the house."

"It's about time!" my father grumbled.

"Do you think we'll have school tomorrow?" I asked.

"Turn on the radio," my mother said, scooping coffee into the electric percolator.

". . . And in Detroit, the will of the late Marjorie Cutler, who died recently, was read today. Miss Cutler left her entire estate, valued at over a million dollars, to her Siamese cat, Princess."

"Isn't that funny?" I said. "We were just talking about millionaires. But why would anyone leave a cat a million dollars? That's dumb. What could a cat do with a million dollars?"

"Move to Florida," said my father glumly.

# IX

A LL RIGHT, class," Mrs. Friedman said, "your homework for the weekend is —"

"Aww," everybody groaned. Homework on a weekend is one of the crummiest ideas teachers have. Homework on a week day is bad enough, but at least it only louses up one evening. On a weekend it louses up three nights and two days, because if you don't do it right away Friday afternoon (and who wants to come home Friday afternoon and do homework?) you *think* about having to do it all through Friday night, Saturday and half of Sunday, and it ruins whatever else you're doing while you're not doing the homework. And when you finally *do* get to it, on Sunday night, your parents stand over you and say, "Why do you always leave things for the last minute? You had *all weekend* to do it. . . ." At least mine say that.

"Your assignment for the weekend," continued Mrs. Friedman, ignoring the groans, "is to write a composition —"

"Yucch," said Kenny Clark.

"— about one of these qualities."

She turned to the blackboard — which is not black, but green, and you're supposed to call it the chalkboard, but only Mrs. Friedman calls it that — and wrote:

# HUMOR
# INTELLIGENCE
# IMAGINATION
# BEAUTY

"Now what I want you to do is pick the quality that you think is most important, and tell me why."

"I don't get it," Kenny Clark said sullenly. "Most important for what?"

"For whatever you want," Mrs. Friedman replied. "That's up to you to decide."

"I still don't get it."

"It can be the quality you think is most important in your own life, or it can be the quality you feel you like most in other people, or the quality you feel is most necessary to be a success in the world. You decide how and why it's important to you."

Spider Webb raised her hand.

"Should it be a quality you have?" She smoothed her hair behind her ear as she lowered her hand. I could see she was eyeing *beauty* and trying to figure out a way to write about being beautiful without sounding even more conceited than she already was. I tried to picture her blown up, like a yellow balloon, puffed out from face to feet with hot air. Then I stuck a pin in her.

"No," Mrs. Friedman said, "as I explained, it can be a quality you admire in somebody else. It all depends on how you approach the idea."

The bell rang.

"How long does it have to be?" Kenny asked as we leaped out of our seats.

"I'm interested in quality, not quantity," Mrs. Friedman said wearily. She must have said that at least fifty times already that year. "Make it as long as it takes to say what you want to say."

"I don't want to say *any*thing," Kenny complained.

Mrs. Friedman ignored him.

"I hate weekend homework," I grumbled to Janey as we climbed onto the bus.

"I hate compositions worst of all," Jane sighed. "I never can think of anything to write."

"Which quality are you going to do?" I asked as we took our seats.

"I don't know," she shrugged. "Who cares, anyway? How do you know what's important? It depends on what you want to be. If you want to be a movie star, beauty's important. If you want to be a scientist, brains are important. It's a dumb assignment."

Spider Webb leaned over the back of our seat.

"I'm writing on Beauty," she announced.

"No!" I gasped, opening my eyes wide. "Really?" She nodded.

"Don't you think you ought to write about something you know from personal experience?" I asked.

"But I *am*," she said patiently.

I think it's impossible to insult someone who refuses to realize she's being insulted. I guess it never occurs to Spider that she's insultable.

"Why don't you write about intelligence?" I suggested, turning back to Jane. "You're intelligent, and besides, that covers everything. I mean, no matter what you want to be, it always helps to be smart."

"Oh, I don't know," Spider said doubtfully.

"I wouldn't expect you to," I said.

Well, like I figured, that composition ruined my whole weekend. I couldn't write it until I figured out what to write about, and I couldn't figure out what to write about. So I kept putting it off until I could think of what quality I was going to write on, and then, suddenly, it was Sunday night.

"I don't understand it," my mother said, watching me sitting at the dining room table, staring at a blank sheet of loose-leaf paper.

"You had *all weekend* to do this. Why do you leave it for the last minute?"

"What are you doing?" I asked nastily, looking pointedly at the book she was writing in.

"My — uh — lesson plan," she said, a little flustered.

"The apple doesn't fall far from the tree," my father remarked, turning on the television.

"When you and your daughter," my mother began, glaring at my father, "take over the cooking and the cleaning, et cetera, et cetera, I will have my lesson plans done three months in advance. Anyway —" she closed the book with a satisfied snap — "*I'm* finished. What are you watching?"

"It's an interview with Charlotte Holland," he said.

My mother settled down on the couch next to him.

"Oh, the one who wrote *The Sins of Silver City?*"

"Right, that's her."

My mother glanced at my father, then looked over at me.

"Um, Vicky, don't you think you'd better work on that up in your room? You won't be able to concentrate with the TV on."

"Oh, that's okay," I said. "It doesn't bother me."

"But, Victory, I really don't see how —"

"What your mother means," explained my father gently, "is 'go to your room.' "

"Good grief," I muttered, gathering up my paper and pen.

I went upstairs and flopped down on my bed, with a book under my paper. I sort of forgot to close the door, so I could still hear the television.

A man was asking Charlotte Holland about this book she had written, which sold so many copies she was now rich and famous.

"You mean to tell me that this book isn't true?" he asked, sounding really surprised.

"Well, I grew up in a town very much like Silver City," the author replied. "But none of the things I wrote about in my book really happened. At least, not that I know of."

"Then you made the whole thing up?"

"Most of it."

I stared at the blank piece of loose-leaf paper in front of me. Sure, I thought, authors don't have this kind of trouble. They just sit down and make things up out of their heads, and before you know it, they've written a whole book, and they sell a million copies and get rich and famous. Now, if I were a writer, one dumb composition would be child's play to me. If I were a writer, I'd . . .

"Okay, Miss Benneker, you're on next." The producer of "The Jerry Griffith Show" patted her shoulder, and pointed toward the opening in the curtain.

"When you're announced, just walk right out and sit down next to Jerry. You're not nervous, are you?"

"Oh, no," she said nervously.

". . . Our next guest, give her a big welcome, Miss Victory Benneker!"

She walked out on stage, and the bright lights in the television studio nearly blinded her.

Victory made her way over to the table where Jerry Griffith sat and slid into the seat next to him.

"Well, Miss Benneker," he smiled, holding up a copy of her book, "so you're the author of this fascinating novel."

"Yes," she said modestly.

"Can I ask you a personal question? How much money have you made from the sales of *The Shame of Oakvale?*"

"Oh, about a million dollars."

"A *million dollars!* Isn't that *fantastic?*"

The audience gasped and applauded.

"Tell me something," he asked confidentially. "Is this a true story?"

"Well, no, not really," she said, beginning to feel less nervous. "Most of it I made up."

"You made it up?" he asked incredulously. "You made up a million-dollar best seller out of your own head?"

Victory nodded.

"What about this character — Beatrice Hive. Bee Hive, you call her." The audience laughed.

"Well, she's based on a real person," she admitted. "But the rest is all my own ideas."

"All these incredible things that go on in Oakvale, all those fantastic people in your book, I can hardly believe one person could have thought up such a — a *fantastic* novel. You must have *some* imagination!"

"I suppose I do," she said simply.

"Fantastic," said Jerry Griffith. "Fan*ta*stic . . ."

Sure, if I. were a famous writer, this composition would be a cinch. A little imagination, that's all it takes.

I sat up on my bed.

But I *do* have imagination, I thought. I must have. How else could I imagine that I was a famous writer? I must have a *lot* of imagination. Why, I could even feel the heat of the television lights, and how nervous I would be — I could even hear the applause. Now, if *that* isn't imagination . . .

I turned over onto my stomach and began to write.

*Imagination*
*by*
*Victory Benneker*

"All right, class, I've marked your compositions. Some of you did very well. Others — well, I'm afraid some people just didn't seem to understand what this assignment was all about."

Mrs. Friedman started handing back our papers.

"Aww — she gave me a D," Kenny Clark grumbled.

Mrs. Friedman stopped next to his desk.

"No, Kenneth," she said cheerfully. "*She* didn't give you a D — *you earned* a D."

She finished handing out the papers. Everybody got their paper back — except me. She was holding one paper in her hand — it must be mine!

Oh, no, I thought. I got an F and she's going to tell everybody what a lousy composition it was, and she'll read it, and then she'll hand it back to me, and everyone will know how rotten I did.

I tried to sort of hunch up in my seat, making myself as small and unnoticeable as possible. But Judy Olivera and Jane, who sat near me, could see that I didn't have anything on my desk, so they knew I hadn't gotten my composition back. Jane lifted her eyebrows at me questioningly.

"I want you to hear one paper," Mrs. Friedman said, "that really stood out from the rest."

I looked up in surprise. She couldn't mean it stood out because it was so *lousy*. Could she?

"When I gave you this assignment, this composition," she waved my paper in the air, "is really what I had in mind."

I began to sit up straighter in my chair.

"Victory, will you read this out loud, please?" She held the paper out toward me as I slowly walked to the front of the room.

She handed me my composition, and I smiled with relief as I saw the big red A+ on the top.

I turned to face the class and nervously cleared my throat.

"Imagination. By Victory Benneker. Imagination is one thing that makes man different from animals. A mouse can't imagine he's a lion, but a person can imagine he's anything he wants to be. If you have a bad day, you can imagine what it will be like when you have a good day. If you're afraid to do something, you can imagine what it's like to be brave enough to do *anything*."

Kenny Clark snickered. "Chicken Vicky," he hissed.

"Kenneth — any more of that and we'll have you read *your* composition so the class can hear what a D paper sounds like."

Kenny slumped down in his seat.

"Whatever you want in life," I continued reading, "is right there in your head. You can be rich, famous, anything you ever dreamed of, just by using a little imagination.

"Imagination is important, and not just for dreaming things up in your head. All the great books that were ever written were thought up in somebody's imagination. Somebody had to imagine the airplane before it was invented. Somebody had to imagine the telephone before Alexander Graham Bell actually made one. Everything that was ever invented or created by man had to be dreamed up in someone's imagination.

"So no matter what you want to be, or what you want to have, you have to imagine it first. Because imagination isn't only fun. It's something you *need* all through your life.

"As a matter of fact, if it weren't for imagination, I never could have written this composition. The End."

"Thank you, Victory," Mrs. Friedman said.

I walked back to my desk. Judy Olivera was staring at me like she didn't recognize me. Jane looked at me like I was suddenly an entirely different person. Mark Vogel was frowning and nodding his head. Kenny Clark was balancing a pencil on the toe of his shoe.

"You see," Mrs. Friedman said, "what Victory did was to describe a quality, and explain what the quality was, how it worked, and what makes it important to people. And she wrote about it well — and with imagination! That was exactly what I had in mind when I gave you this assignment. Anybody want to make any comments about this?"

Everybody started buzzing at once.

"Yes, Mark?"

"It's true, what she said. I mean, a man, he can think about being something different, and if he can't be different, no matter how hard he tries, he can always pretend in his mind that he is. I mean — and then maybe, someday, he will be. Different, I mean."

"And you can sort of — daydream," Jimmy Fallon broke in. "I mean, like little kids do, you know — pretend." He sounded sort of embarrassed.

"Not only little kids daydream, Jimmy. Everybody does, sometimes. As Victory said, it's part of being a human being."

I sat straight up in my seat, listening to everyone talking about my composition. A lot of kids were waving their hands in the air, anxious for Mrs. Friedman to call on them. And they were all saying how I was right, and my composition was true, and they knew exactly what I meant.

I didn't say anything. I just sat there. I felt myself smiling and smiling, and I couldn't stop.

The bell rang, and Jane and Judy collected their books and came up to my desk.

"Wow," Janey said, "I've known you almost my whole life, and I didn't know you could write that well."

"Yeah," Judy said. "You must have lots of it — I mean, imagination."

"I guess so," I said.

"You ought to be a writer," Judy said. "I'll bet you'd be famous some day."

"*. . . And they tell me, Victory, that your book has sold a million copies already. Isn't that fantastic?*"

"Yeah," Jane was agreeing, "and we can say we knew you before you were famous, when you were struggling over compositions in the sixth grade!"

"*. . . fantastic!*"